W9-AOQ-326

 # THE TEXAS TATTLER

All the news that's barely fit to print!

Fortune Empires To Merge
International Business Deal Unites Family

Financial newsflash—What do you get when you combine Texas's and Australia's most successful ranching operations? A whole lotta honor, a whole lotta ego and a whole lot *more* money. Wall Street was reeling this week when word leaked that the mammoth Double Crown and Crown Peak ranches will merge, creating the single largest ranching outfit in history. *Investors, Inc.* says "Fortune" is now *the* name in ranching.

The deal will skyrocket the Fortune power and wealth to astounding proportions, though it is still too early for solid predictions about the impact on the family's net worth. But one thing's for sure...if these folks keep merging, marrying and mothering at this rate, they're going to give a whole new meaning to Fortune 500!

And on to "love news"...*The Tattler*'s fashion guru couldn't help but notice the sudden, drastic change in Teddy Fortune's only daughter, Matilda. She has traded in her dusty overalls for utterly elegant duds. Could all this focus on her femininity have something to do with exec-to-swoon-for Dawson Prescott? A source *amazingly* close to the famed family says that Dawson has tried to resist the tomboy-turned-tantalizer, but recent late-night "developments" (involving a boudoir, a shotgun and an ultimatum) might mean one more Fortune will soon bite the marriage dust!

THE FORTUNES OF TEXAS™

 Meet the Fortunes of Texas

Matilda Fortune: From the moment Matilda met Dawson Prescott, he made her heart skip a beat. So the former tomboy transformed herself into a stunning, self-assured woman and hoped the new-and-improved Matilda could win his heart.

Dawson Prescott: When he was found in a compromising position with Matilda, he dutifully married her. Would his new bride turn out to be the perfect wife he hadn't known he was looking for?

Griffin Fortune: The secret agent didn't think of himself as the marrying kind. But when he was asked to protect an innocent beauty, he began to second-guess his bachelor status....

SHOTGUN
Vows

TERESA SOUTHWICK

Silhouette Books

Published by Silhouette Books

America's Publisher of Contemporary Romance

If you purchased this book without a cover you should be aware that this book is stolen property. It was reported as "unsold and destroyed" to the publisher, and neither the author nor the publisher has received any payment for this "stripped book."

Special thanks and acknowledgment are given to Teresa Southwick for her contribution to THE FORTUNES OF TEXAS series.

SILHOUETTE BOOKS

ISBN 0-373-21747-1

SHOTGUN VOWS

Copyright © 2001 by Harlequin Books S.A.

All rights reserved. Except for use in any review, the reproduction or utilization of this work in whole or in part in any form by any electronic, mechanical or other means, now known or hereafter invented, including xerography, photocopying and recording, or in any information storage or retrieval system, is forbidden without the written permission of the editorial office, Silhouette Books, 233 Broadway, New York, NY 10279 U.S.A.

All characters in this book have no existence outside the imagination of the author and have no relation whatsoever to anyone bearing the same name or names. They are not even distantly inspired by any individual known or unknown to the author, and all incidents are pure invention.

This edition published by arrangement with Harlequin Books S.A.

® and TM are trademarks of Harlequin Books S.A., used under license. Trademarks indicated with ® are registered in the United States Patent and Trademark Office, the Canadian Trade Marks Office and in other countries.

Visit Silhouette Books at www.eHarlequin.com

Printed in U.S.A.

About the Author

TERESA SOUTHWICK

At the tender age of ten, Teresa Southwick learned to deal with rejection when her four brothers found and "critiqued" one of her medieval stories. Then she could tattle to Mom, who unfortunately didn't send the blackguards to the gallows, or at the very least the dungeon, as Teresa had hoped. But it would be almost thirty years before she would again put pen to paper—or more accurately, fingers to keyboard.

A California girl born and raised, she spent many blissful hours sitting on the beach reading romance novels. Her fondness for happy endings began with Nancy Drew, and if she'd written those stories, Nancy and Ned would be living happily ever after. The good news is that her fascination with a wonderful love story was alive, well and flourishing in spite of her brothers.

She sold her first book in 1993, and in 1995, she achieved her longtime goal of writing for Silhouette Romance. The best part of writing, she believes, is that there are always more challenges around the corner. When she was asked to participate in THE FORTUNES OF TEXAS series, she jumped at the chance to write *Shotgun Vows*. The experience of working with such a talented and generous group of writers was both daunting and rewarding. The best part was sharing the news with her brothers—blackguards matured into heroes—who never miss a chance these days to brag about their "famous" sister.

Teresa and her husband have two grown sons.

To THE FORTUNES OF TEXAS authors.
It's been a pleasure and a privilege working with
a talented, generous group of writers.
I'm grateful to be included in your ranks.

One

It was rumored that Griffin Fortune knew three hundred ways to kill with his bare hands. How could you say no to someone like that?

"You're absolutely sure you want me to watch out for your sister?" Dawson Prescott asked again.

He studied Griffin, sitting across the desk from him. Dawson wasn't afraid of him; he was a friend. In spite of Griff's dangerous reputation, Dawson liked him and his brothers. It was their sister, Matilda, who rubbed him the wrong way.

Griff brushed a hand over his dark brown hair. The short, military cut didn't move. "You heard me right," he said. His Australian drawl did nothing to soften the words. If anything, his "down under" accent added intimidation. "I want you to watch over Mattie while I'm gone. We had this discussion already."

"Yeah, I remember," Dawson said. "I just didn't think you were serious." *Hoped* he wasn't serious would be more accurate. But Dawson suspected Griff never said anything he didn't mean.

"Dead serious," he answered, confirming the suspicion. "If I could put off this job, I would." He met Dawson's gaze squarely and a predatory glint crept into his brown eyes. "But I have to go."

Dawson knew he would say no more about it than that.

Here in the plush carpeted, wood-accented office at Fortune TX, Ltd. where he worked as a financial analyst, it was hard for Dawson to imagine what the other man did when he disappeared. But Dawson had quickly come to like and respect him. Whatever it was that took the man out of town, Dawson instinctively knew Griffin Fortune was one of the good guys.

Dawson pushed his cushy leather chair away from the desk, leaned back, and linked his hands over his abdomen. "But again I have to ask—why me? My baby-sitting skills leave something to be desired."

"If she were a baby, we wouldn't be having this conversation," Griff said, his Aussie drawl thickening with irony.

As much as he wanted to, Dawson couldn't argue with the fact that Matilda Fortune was no baby. Every time he heard her name, he instantly thought of her long, shapely legs encased in denim—followed quickly by a flash of those legs wrapped around his waist. He'd only ever seen her in work clothes with her shirt pulled out and hanging loose. If the rest of her was as good as those legs, and he ever got a look at the package, they would all be in trouble.

The weird thing was that in the looks department she was nothing to write home about. Ordinary braided blond hair, average gray eyes, and pale skin all added up to a woman as plain as her name: Matilda. Who thought that up? Dawson only knew that she pushed some of his buttons—all of them wrong. But it was unlikely that anything personal would ever happen with her. Ever since they had laid eyes on each other, sparks had flown between them—and not the good kind.

"Correct me if I'm wrong," he said, "but isn't she twenty-one? Why does she need looking after?"

"She's been sheltered. She trusts everyone and has never met a stranger. My four brothers and I have always watched out for her. But she's changed since she got to Texas. What do you people put in the water?"

Dawson blinked. "Excuse me?"

"There's something going around and it's called Matrimony. Seems to be catching. Soon my brother Brody and Jillian will be tying the knot. But it all started with my brother Reed when he married your sister."

Dawson and his half sister Mallory hadn't grown up together. Different mothers. But his gut told him his sister's match with Griff's brother was a good one. "I've never seen her happier."

"Reed, too." One corner of Griff's mouth lifted as he sat up straighter in the chair. "On top of that, Mattie's been acting strange ever since she found out that Jillian is going to have a baby. I overheard her tell Jillian that she wants one of her own soon. I wouldn't put it past her to run off with one of the ranch hands at the Double Crown."

Dawson couldn't remember ever hearing Griff string together that many sentences. Obviously the guy was really concerned. With a sister of his own, Dawson could understand the protective instinct. But he was a financial analyst for crying out loud. Granted, he worked for the family company, Fortune TX, Ltd. But surely they wouldn't expect him to nursemaid Matilda Fortune, the troublemaker cousin from Australia.

The assignment was definitely above and beyond the call of duty. He worked on spreadsheets... Bad choice of words. Instantly he thought of Matilda's long legs and tangled bed sheets. Damn, this was a bad idea. He'd agreed reluctantly, and only because he'd never actually expected Griff to take him up on it. Now he wished he'd never said yes.

The question was how he could gracefully get out of this. *Here goes,* he thought ruefully.

"She doesn't like me much, Griff. Surely you've noticed. If looks could kill, I'd be a chalk outline on the floor. Wouldn't it be better if you found someone else for guard duty?"

"There are three things that make you an ideal candidate for this assignment." Dawson didn't miss the harnessed strength in the other man's wrist and forearm as he held up three fingers. "One—Reed is on his honeymoon, and Brody is too preoccupied with his own upcoming wedding and becoming a father in a couple of months to do the job justice. Two—you're practically a Fortune, being my cousin Zane's friend and all. Three—you're right. She hates your guts." He grinned. "That makes you perfect for the job, mate."

"I've got number four."

"What's that?" he asked.

"She's just a kid."

He was eleven years her senior, a fact he'd pointed out at his first meeting with the Australian she-devil. Not that he was old. She'd figured that out all by herself. They'd accompanied Reed and Mallory to the rodeo. All Dawson had said was that he hadn't expected Reed's sister to be so young. That had instantly gotten Matilda's back up, and she'd fired off her own verbal shot.

Even if Dawson were attracted to her—at least the "her" that was separate from those dynamite legs—the disparity in their ages was something he would never get past. After his parents had split up, his father had married a much younger woman—a fact that had angered and embittered his mother. She'd had her nose rubbed in the fact that she was no longer young and had no weapons to fight for her man. Dawson had vowed that he would never use a woman and toss her aside like yesterday's meat loaf. Furthermore, he would never make the same mistakes his father had.

He wasn't like his father. He would never be like him.

Griff nodded. "By process of elimination as well as default, you're the ideal candidate."

Dawson knew he had no choice, and the thought rankled. He wasn't a man who liked being backed into a corner. "How long are you going to be gone?"

Griff shrugged. "There's no way to know for sure. I'll do my best to get back before Brody and Jillian's wedding."

That was just over three weeks away, the weekend before Thanksgiving. Dawson figured he could handle Matilda Fortune that long.

He nodded slowly. "I'll make sure she doesn't run off with a cowboy."

"Good. One favor, Dawson."

"I'm already doing you a favor."

"Then do yourself one. Don't let Mattie know what you're up to."

"She wouldn't like it?"

Griff laughed, but there was no humor in the sound. "That's an understatement. She doesn't like being treated like a kid. She's a grown woman, she says."

"Yeah, that message got through loud and clear," Dawson commented.

"Then if you know what's good for you, don't let on that I asked you to keep an eye on her."

"I'll do my best," he promised.

Satisfied, Griff held out his hand. "I owe you, mate."

And then some, Dawson thought, hoping he wouldn't live to regret this. It was the first of November and the promise he'd made just about guaranteed that he could kiss off having only good days for three-quarters of the month.

Matilda Fortune listened to the *clunk* of her boots on the foyer tile as she made her way to the Double Crown Ranch's great room. She stopped when her heels sank into the thick carpet. The large open hearth held a cheery fire. On the other wall, French doors opened to one of the house's two courtyards. Large leather couches and comfortable chairs in groupings that invited intimate conversation were arranged in several places in the large room.

Since her arrival from Australia several months ago, she found it was her uncle Ryan and aunt Lily's custom to spend the evening in the great room. Tonight was no exception. They were sitting side by side on one of the leather sofas, having after-dinner drinks with their other houseguest, Willa Simms. She was Ryan's goddaughter. Willa's father and Ryan had been best friends in Vietnam, a bond that remained strong until her dad died of cancer. She was still very close to Uncle Ryan—like one of his children.

Through an archway to her right she could see the dining room and the living room beyond. A huge painted armoire, and Western-style pieces including antler lamps and Native American prints, gave the room warmth and personality. She liked the house in spite of its intimidating size and the fact that she always felt as if she brought the outdoors inside as soon as she walked in.

Mattie moved farther into the room until she faced her aunt and uncle. "I didn't see Griff's car outside. Does anyone know where my brother is?"

She knew the answer even as the words came out of her mouth. If Griff's car were here, she would have known his whereabouts. He was joined at the hip with her. Her shadow. Her keeper. If his car was gone, he must be on one of his mysterious trips.

"He left on business, dear," her aunt said, confirming Mattie's guess. "He wasn't sure when he would be back, but asked me to tell you not to worry."

"From his mouth to God's ear." Mattie whispered her usual fervent prayer.

Telling her not to worry was like asking the wind not to blow. Griff would never confide details to anyone in the family about what he did when he was away. He said the less they knew, the better. How could they not worry when someone they loved said *that?*

But she smiled at her aunt and uncle, not wanting to upset them or let anyone know her feelings. There was nothing they could do or say to ease her mind.

Mattie studied her aunt and uncle, thighs brushing while holding hands. As always, she was struck by what a handsome couple they were. She knew they were both in their early fifties, but neither looked it. Lily's eyes were the color of a moonless night, and her shiny black bob, along with the beautiful bone structure in her face, revealed her Spanish and Indian heritage. She was still a lovely woman and must have been a stunner as a young girl.

Uncle Ryan was definitely his wife's equal. With his dark eyes and hair showing a bit of gray at the temples, and a still-muscular physique, he must have made female hearts flutter in his younger days. And at least one female heart still fluttered, Mattie thought as she saw the glow in his wife's eyes as she looked up at him. The two were obviously in love, obviously soul mates.

Like her own parents.

Mattie sighed. Would she ever find someone who would love her like that? A man she could respect and care about and raise a family with? A soul mate of her own?

It was her most cherished dream. Unfortunately, her brothers frightened away anyone who showed even the slightest interest in her. That made it darn near impossible to make her fairy tale come true. If Prince Charming didn't have the guts to face down the Fortune brothers, then she didn't particularly want to set up housekeeping in his castle. No wimp for her!

When her aunt and uncle had visited Australia and invited her to their ranch in Texas, she'd thought it was the opportunity she'd been waiting for. She'd taken them up on the offer and fallen in love with the state, the air, the wide-open spaces. The *men* that all the wide-open spaces would hold.

Since horses were her life, where better to find the man of her dreams than a Texas ranch? So many cowboys, so little time. The bad news was that Griff never left her side. The steely-eyed looks he gave any man who even glanced in her direction were enough to make monks out of them.

But Griff was gone. What was that American saying? *Make hay while the sun shines.* How appropriate on a ranch! And she finally understood the meaning. She would worry terribly about Griff, but with him away, it was definitely hay-making time.

Tonight the Double Crown cowboys held their weekly poker game. She'd almost forgotten, having dismissed the earlier casual reminder because she knew there was no way Griff would let her go. Or worse, he would accompany her—and then no one would have any fun. This was her first chance to join in. Maybe she could finally get one of them to notice her.

"I'm sorry we couldn't hold dinner for you, dear," her aunt said.

"No worries," Mattie answered.

"I just love your accent," Willa chimed in. "It's so cute."

"Thanks." Mattie smiled at her, then looked back at her aunt and uncle. "I'm sorry to be so late. I just couldn't tear myself away."

"Your brothers say you have a way with animals, Mattie," Willa said. "They say when they have a problem horse, you're the one they go to. That's such a gift. I'm a little afraid of an animal big enough to stomp me into roadkill without a second thought."

"You traveled all over the world with your father, Willa," Uncle Ryan said. "There was never time or opportunity to learn about horses."

"I'd be happy to work with you and show you some tricks," Mattie said. "Then you would be more comfortable around them. There's no reason to be afraid of horses. I can find just the right animal—one with a nature as sweet as yours.''

Willa smiled. ''How I envy your ability to do that.''

Not as much as I envy you. Mattie barely held in a sigh. Willa was so petite and pretty. Even her wire-rimmed glasses couldn't disguise her beautiful blue-gray eyes. Tonight her shoulder-length auburn hair was secured on top of her head with a clip. Mattie made a mental note to ask how she did that. All thumbs herself, she never fussed with her hair. A braid was easy, fast, and worked just fine. That clip contraption wouldn't hold up when she was riding. But if she had a date, it could work just fine, she thought.

Lily sipped her brandy. ''Rosita put the leftovers in the fridge for you, Mattie.''

''Thank you.''

Then she was free. No big brother watching. Whatever was she going to do with all this independence? The pressure was on. She didn't know how long Griff would be gone. The possibilities were endless. But tonight there was that poker game. Exhilaration surged through her, lifting her spirits.

The coast was clear!

Rosita Perez, the Fortunes' sixtyish housekeeper, entered the room. Her black hair was pulled back, highlighting the one white streak that started at her forehead and disappeared into the bun at her nape. Mattie liked the motherly woman who dished out hugs almost as plentifully as food. The downside was that she was followed by a man in business clothes.

Mattie felt two parts excitement and one part irritation when she recognized Mr. Stuffed Shirt in the expensive suit. Dawson Prescott.

He hardly looked at her as he walked briskly past

her to Uncle Ryan and shook hands. He nodded to her aunt and Willa, then gave Mattie the briefest of glances. Boy, that chapped her hide. Just like their first meeting when he had said she looked eighteen. Ever since, he'd ignored her, as if she didn't exist. Every time she'd seen him around the Double Crown with her cousin Zane and her brothers, he hadn't even glanced her way. *Cheeky devil,* she thought. She tried not to let it bother her, but it damn well did.

"I brought the portfolios for you to look at, Ryan," he said to her uncle.

"Didn't I tell you that I trust your judgment? I've put together a dynamite staff, the best there is, one that I trust implicitly to handle money matters. Mostly family, I might add." He looked at Dawson. "Or practically family."

His wife smiled lovingly at him. "Didn't anyone ever tell you that pride, even in staff that is practically family, goes before a fall, my darling?" she teased.

He put his arm around her. "Yes. And when mine comes, it'll be a humdinger. I can only hope there's a bungee cord attached when it happens. But I trust Dawson. It wasn't necessary to bring this out here tonight."

Lily looked at the newcomer. "But since you did, the least we can do is feed you. Have you had dinner yet, Dawson?"

Tell her yes, Mattie said to herself. *Yes, yes, yes.*

"No, I haven't," Dawson answered. "But it's not necessary—"

"There are plenty of leftovers," Lily continued. "Can we warm something up for you?"

Say no, Mattie thought. *No, no, no.*

"That would be great," he said. "But I don't want to put you to any trouble."

Perverse man, Mattie thought. Completely ignored her mental telepathy. She would have to work on that.

"It's no trouble, dear," Lily said. "As a matter of fact, Matilda just walked in, and she hasn't had dinner yet, either. So now she won't have to eat alone." The older woman smiled brightly.

The evening had just gone downhill in a big way, Mattie decided. And it had started out so promising.... Now she was cornered. She wouldn't insult her family by not extending hospitality to another guest in their home. She would set a record for fast food-consumption, then say her farewells and head for the bunkhouse.

She forced herself to smile at Dawson. "I'm going to go clean up. Then I'll meet you in the kitchen."

"Don't rush, dear," Lily said. "We'll entertain Dawson while you freshen up."

During her shower and then a quick combing and braiding of her hair afterwards, all Mattie could think was, *Why me?* Why did she draw the short straw and get stuck with the dude? Although if she had to be stuck with someone she didn't like, at least he wasn't hard on the eyes. She hadn't been that close to him since their first verbal sparring. Then she'd been too annoyed to notice. But tonight, being in the same room with him, she couldn't miss the intensity that made his hazel eyes seem more green, or the way the light picked up the sunstreaks in his brown hair, or how wide his shoulders looked in that white dress shirt, wrinkled after a day's work.

"Work?" she said to herself, slipping on a clean pair of jeans. "Number cruncher," she said disdain-

fully as she put on a long-sleeved white cotton shirt.
She couldn't think of a more boring or lonely way to
make a living. In fact, she might even feel sorry for
him—if he was anyone but Dawson Prescott.

She glanced one last time in the mirror, and sighed
as she noticed the blond wisps of hair that curled
around her face. No matter how hard she tried, her
hair had a mind of its own. So she'd quit trying to
make it do anything other than braid. Was it her imagination, or did her eyes look a deeper gray than usual?
Must be the anticipation of that poker game, she
thought.

Mattie made her way to the kitchen. The floor of
the large room was tiled with Mexican pavers. A dis-
tressed-wood table with eight ladder-back chairs stood
in a cozy nook at one end of the room. At the other
end was a center island work area, a counter cooktop
set into the cream-colored tiles, and a built-in oven.
Not to mention the largest side-by-side refrigerator she
had ever seen.

That was where she now saw Dawson, half bent at
the waist as he scoped out the contents. She noticed
that his gray slacks pulled tight across his legs, revealing muscular thighs. She wondered how he managed to produce all those muscles while poring over
numbers all day.

"See anything good?" she asked.

"Lily and Ryan said to make myself at home," he
answered, as he continued to study the interior.

Then he looked at her, and she thought his gaze
lowered to just about her knees. No doubt he was trying to think of something to say to cut her off just
about there. She resolved not to rise to any bait he

might set out. She would be the lady her mother always scolded her into trying to be.

She pointed to the open door. "I think pot roast and mashed potatoes were on tonight's menu. If you'll allow me?"

He backed away with an outstretched palm. "Be my guest."

"Actually, I believe you're *my* guest."

"Look, Matilda—"

She held her hand up, palm out. "Stop right there, buster." She tried to add a teasing note to her voice. "My aunt expects us to keep each other company for this meal. That implies making conversation. To do that you need to get my attention. Especially if I have my back turned. I'll answer to 'Hey, you,' or 'Yo, babe.' You can even grunt if you'd like. But I despise being called Matilda. I let my family get away with it sometimes. But never ever, under any circumstances, call me that. Mattie is fine. Tildie will do. But if you call me Matilda, life as you now know it will cease to exist."

"Tilde?" He stepped back so that she could pull the leftovers from the refrigerator. "That funny little sideways squiggle used in words to indicate nasality? Or in logic and mathematics to show negation?"

She was pulling two leftover dishes out, but stopped to shoot him an impatient glance. "I thought you had more to do at work."

"How's that?"

"You must have a lot of time on your hands if you can remember such useless, insignificant information. How do you do it?"

"It's a gift," he said with a shrug. "But I could ask

you the same thing. How do *you* do it? Training horses is a lot of work.''

She thought about that as she took two plates and put meat, potatoes, gravy and string beans on them, then put them in the microwave to warm. Then she turned to look at him. ''I can't explain it. I just love animals—especially horses. I study their body language and mentally file away their disposition and character. They have traits, you know. Just like people.''

''So you sort of do what I do. Tuck information away in your head. Some of it useless, some of it not,'' he said.

Damn the man. He had her there. Aunt Lily was right. Pride did indeed go before a fall. Her mother was right. She should behave like a lady and be gracious. She would eat a lot less crow that way.

''I guess you're right,'' she said as sweetly as possible. ''But you've had so many more years than I've had to gather information. How do you remember it all?''

He folded his arms over his chest. A very impressive chest, she noted with a small surprising flutter of her heart.

''A world-class memory,'' he said, one corner of his mouth lifting. ''And fortunately, I'm not ready to take up residence in the geriatric ward yet.''

''I'm sorry. I didn't mean it that way. It's just that what you do boggles the mind. I've never been very good with numbers myself. I'm in awe of anyone who can make sense of it.''

''A lot of what I do is guesswork and instinct. Just like you,'' he said.

She grinned. "But I bet your numbers don't give you love and affection like my horses do."

He laughed. "You win that round. But I have no emotional investment in my numbers the way you do your horses. They can't break my heart."

She saw a black look in his eyes. A remembered pain? She would have sworn that's what it was, and in spite of who he was and how he tweaked her temper, she did feel sorry for him.

"Who broke your heart?" she asked, automatically softening her tone as if she were working with one of the horses.

Instantly the vulnerable expression was gone, replaced by a teasing grin. "What makes you think someone broke my heart?"

"Mother says a person doesn't get through life without some heartbreak. And you've lived so very, very long," she said teasingly. "Surely there are skeletons in your closet."

"Only on Halloween."

"Isn't there a saying in your country—no pain, no gain?"

"I think I've heard that one." He shrugged. "Either I'm emotionally backward, or I've managed to gain without the pain part. What about you? Was your mother right? Have you had your heartbreak in the year-and-a-half you've been on this earth?"

"Cute. I'm not that young." What she was was inexperienced, thanks to her brothers. Except for one single, painful episode. But a stampede of determined Texas mustangs couldn't force her to share the details of that humiliation with him.

"From where I'm standing, you look hardly more than a baby."

Her back started to rise at his comment, making her want to show him that she was a full-grown woman. Her next thought was that he'd turned the conversation away from himself and back to her. Interesting. The words were spoken in a joking manner, but she sensed currents of emotion in him. *Had* someone broken his heart? Or was his pain from something else? She instinctively knew that if she asked, he would put her off.

Instead she watched him, mostly his eyes, then noted the tension in his square jaw. Noted also that he was a very good-looking man, in an older, businessman sort of way. Her heart began to beat very fast, and she grew warm all over. She hadn't felt this way but once, when she *had been* hardly more than a baby. Barely sixteen, she'd managed to elude her brothers long enough to develop a crush on a boy. The incident was a disaster.

But Dawson was a man—the first she'd ever been alone with as a woman. Surely that was the reason her body responded this way when she was near him. That, and the fact that she was *ready* to become a woman in every way. She'd been ready for a long time, but she had way too many brothers who took turns never letting their guard down. The explanation for her reaction to this man had to be that simple. Because Mr. Prescott was absolutely not her type.

But one thought struck her above everything else: her uncle Ryan's comment about his "dynamite" employees. She had a feeling that if she wasn't careful, this particular very male employee could light her fuse and blow up her whole world.

Two

Dawson helped Mattie set silverware and napkins on the table. When the microwave signaled that the food was warm, she grabbed a pot holder and took the plates to the table. They sat down at a right angle to each other, and she began to shovel food into her mouth as if she hadn't eaten for a month.

"Where's the fire?" he asked.

"Pardon?" she answered. Her gray eyes—very pretty eyes he couldn't help noticing—met his gaze. Then she resumed eating.

"You're going to have indigestion if you don't slow down."

"No worries. I've got the constitution of an elephant."

Not exactly the way he would describe her, Dawson thought ruefully. Those legs. He would bet every last penny of his considerable annual bonus that her gams were not thick and wrinkled and gray. If they were, he was sure the knot in his gut would disappear. Considering the size of that knot, he had a heck of a nerve warning her about indigestion. Or anything else for that matter.

He wished he'd never agreed to keep an eye on her. Even Ryan had questioned his excuse for dropping over tonight, but it was the best he could come up with. He had to be here to watch her. Long-distance baby-sitting wouldn't cut it—Dawson didn't do anything halfway. Besides, just before he'd left, Griff had reminded him that Clint Lockhart was still loose. He had escaped from prison and eluded all law enforcement efforts. The man had sworn revenge on the Fortunes, and was slippery as an eel. He'd already killed Ryan's second wife Sophia—who knew what he might do next?

Dawson knew that being a Fortune made Mattie vulnerable to Clint. If anything happened to her because Dawson slacked off, he wouldn't want to face her brother. But more important, he would never forgive himself.

Suddenly Mattie put her fork down, apparently finished. She stared at him. "Are you one of those anal-retentive people who chew each bite of food twenty-seven times?"

"No," he said, staring at her. "But I don't swallow it whole, either."

"Wouldn't have figured you for a slow eater. You strike me as the kind of man who has places to go, women to meet etcetera, etcetera."

"Nope."

"Really?" She nervously tapped her fingers on the table. "So no one is waiting for you at home?"

"Nope. I'm all yours."

"Until you finish your dinner." She rolled her eyes and heaved a huge sigh before glancing at the clock on the stove. She frowned. "You want to hurry it up?"

He looked at his watch. Eight o'clock. He got the feeling she was in a rush. "You going somewhere?"

"No," she said with a breezy nonchalance that screamed liar. "But it's getting late. I've heard if you eat too much too late at night, you'll have nightmares. Your body can turn on you if you make it digest all that food when it's supposed to be resting. Especially when you're advanced in years. So if I were you, I'd quit eating before you regret it.''

Since when did she care about his digestion? Not only that, but she was as nervous as a long-tailed cat in a room full of rocking chairs. What the heck was she up to? ''Come clean, Mattie. Tell me what's going on.''

Before she could answer, Lily Fortune walked into the kitchen.

Dawson envied Ryan. Lily was a lovely woman, and Dawson was glad the two had rekindled their love, which had begun when they were teenagers.

''I'm sorry to interrupt,'' she said.

''No worries,'' Mattie answered.

''You're not interrupting,'' Dawson said at the same time.

The older woman smiled at him, then Mattie. ''I just wanted to let you know that Willa's already gone upstairs, and Ryan and I are going to make an early night of it, too. But please make yourselves at home.''

Dawson nodded. ''Thanks.''

''One more thing.'' Lily looked from Dawson to his fidgety dinner companion. ''Mattie, I just remembered something.''

''Yes?''

''Tomorrow a group of schoolchildren are coming to the ranch on a field trip. I think the principal said they were eleven or twelve years old. They won a contest, and their prize is a day of horseback riding on the Double Crown.''

"Can't think of a better reward," Mattie answered enthusiastically.

"I have a favor to ask you. Would you supervise choosing horses for the children? You have such a way with the animals, and the kids couldn't be in better hands than yours."

A sweet smile transformed Mattie's face, making her eyes glow. "I would be happy to, Aunt Lily."

The older woman nodded approvingly. "I understand there will be four or five children. It might be best if you have one of the ranch hands assist you."

The glow in Mattie's eyes turned to a gleam that Dawson didn't trust. He remembered Griff's warning that she was looking to run off with one of the cowboys. Although she'd been working with them on the ranch for some time, Lily had just reminded him how closely. Because of his promise, it was now his problem. He could only think of one solution.

Before opening his mouth, his last thought was that this must be what it felt like to jump out of a skydiving plane. Then he said, "I would be happy to help her."

Mattie, just sipping water, started to cough. Lily patted her on the back. "Are you all right, dear?"

Still coughing, Mattie nodded. Then she stared at him and asked, "You?"

"No, Mel Gibson," he said, hoping to pull this off with humor. "Of course me."

He would have to take the day off. But he'd been working a lot of hours lately, bringing Brody up to snuff on Fortune financial affairs. Dawson had earned himself a comp day. He was meeting Brody at the office in the afternoon. But he could use the morning for baby-sitting detail. To keep her away from the cowboys, he would stick to her like lint to tape.

"Really, that's awfully nice of you." Mattie shot him a look that made a lie of her words. It told him she wished the earth would open and swallow him up. "But one of the ranch hands would probably be more helpful."

"Not necessarily. I've spent a lot of time riding with Zane. I can handle horseback riding basics for kids."

"You don't need me to work that out," Lily said. "I'll say good-night now." She smiled at each of them. "Sleep well, you two."

When they were alone again, Mattie said too sweetly, "Don't you have some numbers to crunch tomorrow? Some minutiae to commit to memory?"

"It can wait."

"You're very generous to offer assistance. But I was thinking of asking Ethan McKenzie."

She'd sure picked someone quick. Maybe she'd had him on her mind all along. For something of a romantic nature? Or an elopement? He couldn't help wondering if Griff was right about her determination to run off with a cowboy. Had she already culled one from the herd, so to speak? All the more reason for Dawson to hang around. Although he had a sneaking suspicion that if he tried to cut the cowboy out completely, she would become even more determined to have him. Not only that, but it could push Dawson into a situation that would tip his hand, and she would figure out that he had promised Griff he'd guard her.

As long as Dawson was around to supervise, he didn't much care who the unfortunate cowboy helper was. "Okay, ask Ethan. But with that many kids, you can probably use more help."

"Probably." She nodded. "Kids can try your patience. They're pretty unpredictable."

"Then you won't mind if I hang around, too."

She looked at him as if he had just said he planned to walk naked from San Antonio to Houston. "Very sporting of you. But I think Ethan and I can handle them. After all, we're both still limber, and practically children ourselves."

"True. An oldtimer like myself has brittle bones. I have to be careful not to break anything. But hasn't anyone ever told you there's no substitute for wisdom and experience?"

"I've heard that. I've seen you riding here on the ranch. But what experience have you had with children?"

"Not much, I'll admit."

"Then give me three good reasons why you would volunteer to put yourself in harm's way with them," she said suspiciously.

"One, maybe it's about time I tried interacting with them. Two, I could be an uncle soon, and kids are still a real mystery to me. And reason number three—if I hang out with kids, maybe I can figure out what makes you tick," he said, watching her face and waiting for the sparks to fly. He wasn't disappointed.

Her gray eyes darkened with something that wasn't quite anger, but was damn defensive. Or maybe it was a defense mechanism. "And why, pray tell, would you want to get to know me better?"

"Beats the heck out of me," he said. "But I do."

Oddly enough, he found that he *did* want to get to know her better. Something about her intrigued him. Her pride. An indomitable spirit that came through loud and clear. She was barely a woman, but he sensed a strength of character beyond her years.

She met his gaze for several moments, gauging him. Finally she said, "I have to give you points for honesty, Mr. Prescott."

"Dawson, please. I feel old enough without you making me feel like my father."

He winced at his own words. After the thoughts he'd had about her, he was hovering way too close to his father's shortcomings as it was.

"All right, Dawson. It's your funeral. But I would appreciate an extra pair of hands. Thanks," she said grinning.

"You're welcome, I think."

She stood. "I'll say good-night then."

"Yeah. I guess it's about that time."

"Oh? And what time would that be?" she asked, the doubtful note in her voice causing her friendly smile to waver.

"Curfew," he answered.

The words produced exactly the effect he'd intended. Her shoulders stiffened, her gray eyes narrowed and finally her full lips thinned. Oddly, he found himself longing to have her sunny smile back.

"I didn't have a curfew even when I should have," she snapped.

"Then what's your hurry? And don't insult my intelligence by saying 'nothing.'"

She peeked over her shoulder as if she were trying to elude surveillance. Then she met his gaze and sighed. "All right. Griff is gone. I suppose it can't do any harm to tell you. It's poker night."

Her brother was right. If she'd known he was a stand-in bodyguard, she would have shut down tighter than a convent school when the fleet was in. "Would you like to expand that explanation a tad?" he asked.

"The ranch hands play poker one evening a week. Tonight's the night. It's an open game. Anyone's invited. I've been dying to learn, but Griff would never let me go. Now's my chance."

"To learn the game?" he asked suspiciously.

"Yes. And get to know the guys better."

"Guys like Ethan McKenzie?"

"Yes."

"The game is open?" When she nodded, he said, "Then no one will mind if I tag along."

He started to walk past her, and she grabbed his arm. "Not so fast, buster. Someone will darn well mind."

"Who?" he asked innocently.

"For starters, me. Why would you want to play poker with a bunch of cowboys? I bet not one of them knows what a tilde is."

"Could be I just want to play poker."

"Yeah, and it could be I'm a high-priced fashion model," she said sarcastically. "Why in the world would you want to spend the evening with a bunch of ranch hands?"

"Like I said before, we haven't had a chance to get to know each other since you've been here. This is as good a time as any."

"For whom?" she asked.

"For me. After all, if I'm going to help you with the kids tomorrow, it seems to me that we would be a more efficient team if we knew each other better."

"We're not a team."

"We will be."

"When snowballs survive in hell," she said.

He ignored her remark and said wistfully, "It's been a long time since I've played poker."

"Why?" She tipped her head to the side and studied him. "Don't you have any friends of your own?"

"Of course I have friends. What would make you ask that?"

"Now that Zane and Gwen are married, you must be pretty lonesome." She gave him an impertinent look.

She thought he needed to make friends? She actually thought Zane Fortune was his only friend? She couldn't genuinely believe that he had no one to hang out with. He cringed at the idea. When Griff got back, they were going to have a long talk about indebtedness. This favor was getting more complicated all the time.

And on top of her zingers, she was actually starting to appeal to him.

"No, I'm not lonesome. I have my spreadsheets to keep me warm," he said. Not to mention thoughts of her long legs.... That image made him hot all over. "I just like to play cards. Okay?" he asked more abrasively than he had intended.

"Even if I'm there?"

Especially if you're there and your brother isn't, he thought. "How can you ask that?" Before she could answer he took her arm and said, "Let's go, Mattie. Seven card stud awaits."

"Huh?"

"No worries," he said, imitating her. "You'll find out."

But he didn't miss the gleam in her eyes at the word *stud.*

* * *

The ranch hands lived in a bunkhouse about three-quarters of a mile from the main house. With Griff around, she'd never had a chance to see the inside. But she'd heard the guys talking, and knew it was Ethan and Bobby Lee's turn to host tonight's poker game. Mattie wanted to jump into the truck she used to get herself around the ranch, but Dawson insisted on walking. It seemed odd to her, since there was a chill November wind blowing. But then, it seemed odd that he was with her at all.

She'd been half joking when she'd said it, but maybe he really *didn't* have any friends. That, along with the fact that he was cooped up inside far too much, pushing around all those numbers, made her feel kind of sorry for him. It could explain why he wanted to hoof it to the bunkhouse. He must have a fresh air deficiency.

It wasn't easy keeping up with his long stride. She was slightly winded by the time they stepped onto the wooden bunkhouse porch. Low voices drifted to them from inside. Now that she was here, Mattie was a little nervous. She was almost grateful that Dawson was with her so she didn't have to walk in alone. It was a bit like going to a school dance with one of her brothers, except that Dawson Prescott would mind his own business and not hers once they were inside. Anticipation chased away her nerves.

She was about to knock, then glanced at him. The light next to the door picked up the angles of his face, making it look rugged and very masculine. And quite attractive. Her heart gave a strange little lurch. When she spoke, her voice was slightly breathless. From their sprint over here, no doubt, she thought. Because she couldn't believe that he was starting to look good to her.

"You don't have to do this if you're tired," she told him.

"On the contrary. I'm looking forward to it." He looked at her uncertainly. "I should warn you about something."

"What?" she asked.

"Cowboys don't like to play cards with a woman."

She gaped at him for a moment, then shook her head. "Surely you can do better than that, Dawson."

He was trying to talk her out of playing. Why? More importantly, why had he suddenly agreed to accompany her? She'd been on the Double Crown for several months, and they'd had little contact. When he'd first suggested coming with her to the game, she'd wondered if, possibly, he was intimidated by Griff and was taking advantage of the fact that her brother was gone to hang out with her. Now she knew she'd been wrong. He was trying to get rid of her. But Matilda Fortune didn't scare easy.

"Seriously, Mattie. Cowboys are superstitious. They think it's bad luck to deal a woman in."

"Then why did they invite me?" She tried to keep her voice level and pleasant. Not easy when she wanted to bop him.

"They're superstitious *and* polite."

"I'm willing to risk it."

"It's your funeral," he said. He shrugged and stuck his hands in his pockets, lifting his suit jacket.

It was a blatantly masculine pose in spite of his sissy suit. That made her wonder what he would look like dressed in jeans and boots, like a cowboy. She had a feeling the image would give her no peace of mind.

"Okay," she answered with an emphatic nod, then rapped on the door.

"Come in." That was Bobby Lee's voice.

Mattie turned the knob and pushed the door inward. She was surprised to see that only three cowboys were there. Ethan and Bobby Lee who shared the cabin, and Burch Picket, a hand who had been hired around the time she'd arrived. They looked up from their cards when Mattie walked in.

She had a quick impression of wooden floors and several bunks. In the corner, there were couches and a couple of chairs in front of a television. The other corner held a small kitchen complete with refrigerator and stove. There was an empty space in the middle because they'd pulled the table into the cabin's main room for the game.

Her gaze rested on dark-haired, brown-eyed Ethan. She knew he was right around her own age, but he looked about seventeen. Even his sunburned face didn't hide the fact that he'd hardly started shaving yet. She thought he was cute, but was vaguely disturbed that being in the same room with him didn't produce any sort of physical response on her part. Not the way being around Dawson did. But that probably had something to do with how angry she'd been the first time she met him, and how he baited her every time he opened his mouth. Ethan seemed like a sweetie, and she just had to get to know him better.

"Hi, guys," she said, greeting all the men.

"What are you doing here, Mattie?" Bobby Lee didn't look too happy. The blond, blue-eyed cowboy's frown was a big clue.

Her heart fell. That wasn't exactly the greeting she'd been hoping for. "It's poker night," she said lamely.

"Yeah." Ethan threw his cards down. "But we didn't think you would—"

"Howdy, stranger." Bobby Lee smiled slowly and stood up, walking toward her. "Been a long time."

"Not that long," she said, confused.

Then she shivered as she felt *him* behind her. She'd momentarily forgotten. *Dawson.* He was so close, and the heat of his body warmed her clear down to her toes. The scent of his cologne tied her stomach in knots. Her heart skipped a beat, kicking her confusion up a notch.

"Yeah, it has been a long time," Dawson answered, reaching out to shake hands with him.

Ethan joined them, just inside the door. "Good to see you," the young cowboy said.

"Goes for me, too. We haven't seen much of you since Zane got married and you quit hanging out here with him." Bobby Lee chimed in. "Dawson, you know Burch Pickett, right?"

"We've met," he said.

The man nodded. "Howdy."

"Ethan, pull up a chair for Dawson."

"What about me?" Mattie asked, hands on her hips.

"Oh, Mattie," Bobby Lee said. There was less warmth in his voice than when he'd greeted Dawson. "I figured you just brought Dawson down here to be neighborly. You're really fixin' t'play cards, are you?"

"That was my plan." She felt about as welcome as the plague.

Ethan pulled over another chair and put it next to

the first. "Here you go, Mattie," he said. "Take a load off, Dawson."

They sat next to each other at the round table, at the center of which sat a bowl of popcorn and another of pretzels. Cards, coins and bills were scattered across the scratched wooden top.

While the men were moving around getting drinks and refilling snack bowls, she whispered to Dawson, "Do you know what the money is for?"

"Betting," he said. "Makes it more interesting."

She would have to take his word on that. She had a bigger problem. "I don't have any money with me. Do you?"

He looked at her as if she had pink hair. "Of course I've got money."

"Can you lend me some? Just until we get back to the house?"

"Okay." He pulled out some folded bills and handed her a couple as he asked, "Do you know anything about poker?"

"Nope. But how hard can it be?" she asked, taking the money.

Ethan handed Dawson a beer and said, "You deal."

"Where's my beer?" Mattie asked, anxious to be a part of the whole thing, to experience everything.

"Are you old enough to drink?" Dawson asked, a twinkle in his eyes. "I'd ask for ID if I were you," he said to Ethan.

"Number one, I'm twenty-one," she said. "Number two, thanks to you, we're on foot and not driving. So who cares if I have a beer?" It annoyed her no end that none of the cowboys moved until Dawson gave them a nod.

"Thanks," she said, when Ethan set the beer can in

front of her. She looked at Dawson. "Now you can deal."

"All right, your ladyship." He looked around at the chuckling men, then his gaze rested on her. She didn't miss the challenge there. With supreme confidence he began shuffling the deck. "Mattie has never played before." The remark produced a series of black looks and barely concealed annoyance. "So let's start with something simple."

That was the Dawson she'd come to know and *not* love. He didn't have to do her any favors. She made a mental note to give him a piece of her mind later. "No need to go easy on me," she said. "I'll pick it up fast."

He smiled, irritating her with the genuine cheerfulness in his look. "All right," he said. "No special treatment." He started to deal, letting the cards land facedown in front of each player. "How about seven card, no peek, roll your own, one-eyed jacks and kings with mustaches wild?" he asked.

Mattie stared at him. "Roll your own? Is this cigarettes or poker?"

"Poker. Do you want me to deal you out?"

"Not on your life," she said, sipping her beer. *Nasty stuff,* she thought. But she would drink the whole can and ask for another before she would let one of them know how much she hated it. "I just have one question. What's this about one-eyed jacks and kings with mustaches?"

Dawson stopped dealing, and quickly riffled through the deck, pulling out the cards in question. He showed her the difference. She nodded. "Thanks," she said. "You can finish now."

He buried the cards to everyone's satisfaction and

completed the job. Without a word, Ethan, who sat on Dawson's right, flipped over his top card. It was a nine of clubs. Then he tossed a dollar into the center of the table. When everyone did the same, she put money in, too. Burch turned over four of his cards, and stopped when he showed a king—clean-shaven, Mattie noticed. He put three dollars on the table, and everyone else did, too. This could get expensive, she thought.

Next Bobby Lee started turning over cards. Since none of them had picked up all their cards, she figured out what "no peek" meant. Then it was her turn. She flipped over four cards before she turned over an ace. She leaned over to Dawson and whispered, "What do I do now?"

"Bet," he answered.

"On what?" she asked.

"You have the highest card showing."

"So I win?" She looked at him.

"Not until all the cards are turned over and we see who has the best hand."

"What's a hand?" She ignored the groans and sighs from the other men.

Dawson patiently explained. "In poker there are hands—a pair, two pair, three of a kind, full house, etcetera up to the highest, which is a royal flush."

She looked down at the table again. "It seems sort of foolish to put money out not knowing if I can win."

"That's part of the fun," he said. "But if you don't want to bet, just say 'check.'"

"Check," she answered.

Dawson turned over all his cards and apparently had nothing, because he said, "I'm out."

They went around the table again. Burch had two kings and two threes—"two pair," someone said.

When it was her turn, she flipped over all her cards and was excited when she saw three aces. All the men groaned.

She looked at Dawson. "Is this good?"

"Yeah. You win," he said. "All the money is yours."

"Really?" This was very exciting. No wonder they did it once a week. She scooped up the bills and coins from the center of the table and returned the money she'd borrowed from Dawson. "Who deals next?" she asked.

Ethan picked up the cards and dealt them. The game moved a bit faster, until Dawson had to explain to her again what constituted a hand and what beat what. There was so much groaning in the room, it sounded like a haunted house on Halloween. And when she won the second round, she felt guilty, and tried not to take the pot. But they insisted, albeit angrily. "Beginner's luck," one of them grumbled.

"Now who deals?" she asked.

Bobby Lee yawned. "It's gettin' pretty late."

Mattie glanced at the clock. It was only nine-fifteen.

Burch stood up. "I gotta get goin'. See y'all later." Faster than you could say "lickety-split," he was gone.

Ethan yawned again and said, "I have to be up early."

"Me, too," Bobby Lee said.

Mattie was confused, a state of mind that was becoming increasingly familiar to her the more time she spent in the company of men who were *not* her brothers. From all she'd heard, these games went on until the wee hours. This seemed very early to break up. And she had just been getting the hang of it. Was

Dawson right about the guys feeling that she was bad luck? Or were they miffed because she had all the *good luck?* Poor sports! She almost blurted that out, but decided against it.

"Guess we'd better go and let these guys get some shut-eye," Dawson said. He curved his hand around her arm and pulled her to a standing position with him.

She noticed that Ethan didn't waste any time opening the door. The chill wind blew in, but it wasn't as cold as the room had been when she'd raked in the last pot. Still, she figured she could be gracious and not let on that she knew they were upset because she'd won. Having so many brothers had taught her a lot about male pride.

"You're right. I have to get up early, too," she said, making her way to the door. "I almost forgot. Aunt Lily asked me to supervise some schoolchildren who are coming to the ranch tomorrow. She suggested that I pick someone to help me with them. How about it, Ethan?" she asked, looking up at him. He was tall and lanky. Not unattractive, but not muscular like Dawson....

She wondered where that thought had come from. It was followed quickly by a fervent hope that this sudden hang-up she'd developed of comparing all men to Dawson Prescott was something she'd get over soon.

"Sure, Mattie," Ethan said. "I'll give you a hand. If Mrs. Fortune wants me to," he answered.

"Good," she said. "I'll see you in the corral around nine-thirty." She thought Dawson mumbled something. "What did you say?"

"I said, let's go and let these guys get some sleep."

Dawson took her elbow none too gently and guided her off the porch.

They started walking toward the big house. Mattie was vaguely disturbed at the abrupt way the evening had ended. Since Dawson had witnessed everything, she decided to risk asking him. "Did it seem to you that the guys were bad sports?"

In the moonlight, she read the wry look he gave her. "Why do you say that?"

"Because I've been around long enough to see them drag to work after a late night of poker. They don't let an early-morning wake-up call stop them—if they're winning. Do you think they were upset because I had some beginner's luck?"

He shook his head. "Nope. It's the female thing."

She stared at him. "Define 'female thing.'"

"Bad luck to play cards with a girl."

"Then why deal me in at all? Or why mention the game in front of me?"

He shrugged. "You're the boss's niece. They couldn't very well tell you to go home."

"I just wish they'd been honest."

Their shoulders happened to brush at that moment and she felt him flinch—or abruptly pull away from the contact. She wasn't sure which. Before she could puzzle it out, they arrived at her front door.

This was the first time a man had ever escorted her home. That thought produced a nervous sort of feeling in the pit of her stomach. But this was Dawson.

"If I'm bad luck, then you won't want to help me with the kids tomorrow."

"I'll risk it," he said. "An honorable man doesn't go back on a promise."

"Suit yourself," she said and went inside.

She leaned against the door and thought again about how Dawson reminded her of dynamite. The more time she spent in his company, the closer the match got to her fuse.

Three

The next morning, Dawson leaned against the corral fence and watched Mattie walk toward him, up the slight hill, from the house. She was surrounded by four kids—a girl and three boys. He wondered what the sassy Aussie would say when he told her Ethan wouldn't be joining them. After clearing it with Lily Fortune, he had volunteered his services so that the young cowboy could better use his time on another chore. Oddly enough, he had derived great satisfaction from taking Ethan out of the equation, but wasn't exactly sure why.

Ditto on the fact that he was anticipating Mattie's explosive reaction to the news. That's what a woman did when her plans didn't pan out. He'd learned that the hard way. He'd been raised by a mother who'd been dumped for a younger woman, so bad news had been abundant. His mother had become increasingly depressed and bitter—a natural reaction when the man she loved had married an adolescent.

It made him determined not to use any woman and then throw her away. It had also taught him skills to deal with an unhappy female. So he had no qualms about giving Mattie the bad news about Ethan. But before he fired the first salvo for World War III, he enjoyed the sway of her hips and her graceful long-legged stride. He noticed the sparkle in her gray eyes and heard her merry laughter after she bent her head and listened to one of the boys. Dawson remembered Griff saying that she'd never met a stranger. He could see the evidence for himself. She'd just met these kids, and she had them eating out of her hand.

He knew that wouldn't be happening if she didn't like kids. And he recalled the other thing Griff had warned him about: she wanted to have a baby. Soon. No matter how ticked she was that he'd canceled out Ethan, it couldn't be as bad as her brother's reaction if she ran away with the wet-behind-the-ears cowboy.

Mattie spotted him and stumbled slightly. Then the group continued on until she and her cowboy wannabes stood in a semicircle around him. The kids gave him odd looks, as if they'd been warned about him. She gave him an appraising glance. *Saucy.* The word described perfectly the way she was eyeing him. And it made him feel like he was a prize quarter horse ready to be put to stud.

Two could play that game. "Something wrong, your ladyship?" he asked, lifting one eyebrow.

"You tell me. Who are you and what have you done with Dawson Prescott?"

He looked down at his scuffed brown boots, worn jeans, and long-sleeved, white cotton shirt. "What's wrong?"

"For starters, you're not wearing your uniform. Where's the white dress shirt, pin-striped suit, red power tie, and loafers with tassels?"

"First of all, I draw the line at loafers with a tassel. Too froufrou. As for the rest, it's hanging in the closet at home in Kingston Estates."

"Ah." She nodded. "The large planned community in San Antonio for the fabulously wealthy."

"You make it sound like a communicable disease."

"If only it were," she sighed.

He glanced down at his boots. "I repeat, is there something wrong?"

"You just look different this way."

"Different good? Or different bad?"

"Different as in less like a stuffed shirt."

"Well, thank you, I think, your ladyship," he said dryly.

She thought he was a stuffed shirt? If he wasn't on assignment for Griff Fortune, he'd show her a thing or two about stuffed shirts. But the fact was that he was here to fend off the other guys, not to teach her anything about men.

She looked around. "I wonder where Ethan is. It's almost ten. I did tell him nine-thirty."

"Actually you told him *around* nine-thirty. I talked to the foreman. He said he needed him for a job. Since I'm here to assist you with your charges, it didn't seem necessary to replace him." He glanced at the kids. The boys were eyeing him as if he had just torched their baseball card collection, and the little girl openly stared at him as if he walked on water. "I'm your only backup."

"That's too bad," she said. "I was looking forward to spending some time with him."

He felt only a slight twinge of guilt for his part in producing her disappointed look. At least, he thought it was guilt. It couldn't be jealousy. He wasn't interested in Mattie that way. Even if she were his type, she was too young. All he cared about was fulfilling his promise to her brother and getting himself off baby-sitting detail. If she found the cowboy type she was looking for, it wouldn't be on his watch.

But her reaction surprised him. Disappointment was a far cry from the explosion he'd expected. He wasn't sure if that was good or bad.

And it didn't much matter. If they got this show on the road pronto, maybe he could get in a couple of hours at the office later.

"So where do we start?" he asked.

"How about introductions." She looked around at the kids and her gaze rested on the small redheaded girl with cornflower-blue eyes. "Ladies first. Katie Mansfield, meet Dawson Prescott."

He held his hand out and the girl, who looked about eleven years old, put hers into his palm, squeezing with a surprising strength. "Miss Mansfield, it's a pleasure to meet you."

"And this motley macho male crew are Nate Howe, Juan Castaneda, and Kevin Dolan." She pointed to a tall, skinny blonde, then a husky dark-haired, black-eyed boy and a chubby guy with unruly brown hair. The boys appeared to be about the same age as Katie.

One by one, they shook hands with Dawson. "It's nice to meet you," he said.

"Now we need to find you just the right mounts," Mattie said. "C'mon, mates."

She lead the way toward the barn, and Dawson's gaze was pulled to the feminine grace of her walk. The hem of her plaid shirt hitched up a notch, and he got a better look at her curvy rear end. He couldn't help wondering if she had a small waist and shapely hips to go with those dynamite legs. All the Matilda images he'd been fighting against—legs wrapped around his waist, twisted sheets and bodies entwined—flooded his consciousness with a vengeance.

All those thoughts were at odds with her fresh-scrubbed face and the long blond braid hanging down her back. She was just a kid. And he was her chaperone—not her Casanova. He was abruptly drawn back to the present by a persistent tugging.

"Don't you just love her accent?" Katie asked Dawson. She took his hand and tugged him forward.

"I do," he answered. Oddly enough, he meant it.

Inside the barn, Mattie walked down the hay-strewn aisle between stalls. She looked from side to side, tapping her lips thoughtfully. Stopping beside one, she said, "Juan, this one is for you. His name is Buck." She continued on until she came to a black, beige, and white pinto. "Katie, this is Buttercup. She has a disposition as sweet as yours."

Dawson watched her pick out two more mounts for Kevin and Nate. Then she grabbed a bridle, handed it to him, and said, "Mr. Prescott is going to demonstrate bridling a horse."

She tapped her lip again. "He'll show you on Buttercup. She's very patient, but—" she gave the kids a serious look "—you must be very gentle with the animals. Treat them the way you would like to be treated. You don't like it if someone punches or slaps you. Right?"

Kevin nodded. "Juan and Nate do that to each other all the time when we line up at school."

Mattie glanced at the two who looked guilty. "But you're not going to do that now. Are you, guys?"

"No," they said in unison.

She looked at him. "Mr. Prescott, you're on."

"Dawson." He looked at the kids. "It's all right to call me by my first name."

Mattie met his gaze. "He thinks Mr. Prescott makes him sound old," she said conspiratorially to the kids.

"He *is* old," Nate said.

"Do you think so?" she said, eyeing Dawson critically. "I guess you just have to get to know him. He doesn't look so ancient to me."

Dawson gritted his teeth. He had no problem being gentle with Buttercup, but there was a certain smart-mouthed female who could use a dressing-down. He wasn't ancient. But the part of him that disconnected from his wounded ego acknowledged that the kid was right. Compared to Mattie, he *was* old.

He congratulated himself on controlling his temper, while Mattie led the way as they walked back to the multicolored Buttercup's stall. When they stopped in front of the mare, she looked at the group with sweet, gentle brown eyes. Dawson hated to admit it, but Mattie was right to pick this animal to demonstrate on. Not only that, but being familiar with all the horses in the barn, he knew each one she'd chosen was sweet-natured and pliable. He realized why Lily Fortune had asked her to supervise the schoolkids. Mattie knew her stuff. And she was as good with the kids as she was with horses.

"Okay, listen up, you guys—and ladies," he added. He didn't miss Katie's pleased smile. Too bad his charm didn't work to tame a certain impertinent Australian miss. "I'm going to show you how this is done, but before you try it, there's something you have to do. Anyone have a clue what it is?"

"Get a ladder for Katie?" Juan said to a round of laughter from his friends.

"No." Dawson looked at each one in turn, but they all shrugged and shook their heads. He met Mattie's gaze, and the sparkle in her eyes told him she knew what he had in mind. "Do you want to tell them?" he asked her.

She nodded. "You must get to know the animal before you try to do anything. These horses are used to a lot of different people riding them, and they're okay with that. But not all animals are that way."

"How do we get to know them?" Nate asked Dawson.

"Have you ever heard the expression that the way to a man's heart is through his stomach?" Four pairs of eyes looked back at him blankly. Maybe he was more ancient than he'd thought. When he looked into the fifth pair of eyes, he saw laughter. The merriment made Mattie's eyes very beautiful. The look made him very warm.

"What Dawson means is that you can make friends with the animals by feeding them, gently touching them and talking quietly to them. They respond best to gentle kindness, not fear and intimidation. After he shows you how to bridle Buttercup, I'll show you where the carrots are kept for feeding the horses. But before we do that, I'll show you how it's done so that you don't get your fingers nipped." She smiled sweetly at Dawson. "Please continue, professor."

Oh, good, he thought. Not teacher, but professor. She just had to make him feel that much older. He spread the leather strips so that they could see the configuration and how it would fit around the horse's face.

"This metal part, called a bit, goes in the horse's mouth. If you haven't made friends with the horse, no way will the animal open up willingly. Consequently, no way will you get it in. Observe." He patted the horse's neck and crooned to her. Then he put the bit in front of her, and she opened her mouth. He used his palm to push it until she allowed it to settle behind her teeth. "Voilà," he said.

Kevin scratched his head, which didn't do his unruly brown hair any favor. "What does walla mean?"

"It means he did it easy as pie," Mattie explained. "Did you notice the way Dawson pushed the bit in with his palm? He kept his fingers out of the way. Horses can get confused and bite. They don't mean to hurt you, but it can happen if you're not careful."

"You mean accidentally?" Katie asked.

"Exactly," Mattie answered, as if the little girl were a star pupil. She moved to the other side of the horse and glanced at Dawson. He thought there was approval in her eyes. Obviously she was surprised that he'd passed her bridle test. He knew that's why she'd asked him to show the kids how it was done. He was glad he'd favorably surprised her.

Mattie patted Buttercup's neck. "For safety purposes, when you give them carrots, keep your palm flat and your fingers out of the way. Buttercup would feel awful if she hurt you."

"How do you know that?" Juan asked.

"I can see it in her eyes." She hugged the horse for a few seconds. "All right. Dawson, you take Katie and Juan. I'll take Kevin and Nate, and we'll get the horses bridled and saddled. Meet you in the corral."

"Right," he said.

About twenty minutes later, they were gathered in the picket-fenced enclosure. All four kids were mounted on their horses.

"Giddyap, horse," Kevin said, moving his body in a forward motion.

"Hold on, buckaroo. I need to adjust your stirrups." Mattie smiled up at the young boy sitting on the horse.

"You need to stick your feet in there. If they flap around like wet noodles, it could scare the horse. If the horse is scared, she might run away with you. If she runs away with you, you'll be scared. If you're scared, I'm scared. If—"

"Okay, Mattie," Kevin grinned. "I get it. I'll hold my horse while you fix the stirrups."

"Good choice. All of you hold your horses until Dawson and I make sure the stirrups are adjusted to fit you. Okay?"

"No worries," they said together.

She laughed, and Dawson grinned, too, watching her. She was wonderful with them. Patient and reasonable. The kids responded in kind. Why was she so *un*reasonable when it came to him?

When everyone was secure, Dawson saddled a horse for himself and one for Mattie. He led them into the corral, where she watched and instructed as the four rode slowly around the perimeter. She and Dawson mounted up.

"All right, kids. I think you're ready. We're going to see how you do out in the open. This is going to be an adventure."

"Truer words have never been spoken," Dawson muttered, watching her trim back as he followed her out of the corral.

"Jillian, I can't thank you enough for coming with me."

"It's my pleasure to show you the sights of San Antonio." Jillian tucked a strand of straight blond hair behind her ear.

Mattie smiled at her soon-to-be sister-in-law across the table. It was hard to believe just that morning she'd been teaching kids to ride in the wide-open spaces of Texas. And now, eight hours later, she was taking in the newest "in club" in San Antonio. She turned her head from side to side, trying to see everything at once.

She noticed the sawdust-covered floor, saloon-style bar, and old-fashioned Western lanterns sitting on the round tables. Anticipation hummed through her. The most impressive sight was the multitude of men bellied up to the bar, boots hooked on the stools.

"So this is the famous Watering Hole, bar and nightspot extraordinaire," she said.

"This is it." Jillian shifted uncomfortably on the wooden, barrel-backed chair. "This is where single women come to meet single men—cowboys hang out here in...droves, so to speak."

"I already noticed the cowboys. It's so exciting. And about time, thanks to my brothers. I feel as if I've missed out on so much. Maybe I can see a little big-city nightlife without my shadow hovering over me."

"You shouldn't be so hard on Griff, Mattie. He loves you and is trying to protect you."

"I know he means well. They all do. But there are so many of them. I thought when I came to Texas, I would have the freedom of a single woman. But every time I turn around, I trip over one of the Fortune boys. Why can't they just let me live my life?"

"Maybe if I'd had a big brother watching over me, I wouldn't have made so many mistakes." Jillian sighed, a big, gusty, sad sound.

Mattie felt guilty and ungrateful for complaining. Truthfully, she didn't know what she would do if anything happened to one of her brothers. Impulsively, she reached across the table and squeezed the other woman's hand. She envied Jillian Hart Tanner's petite, pretty, blond good looks. Next to her, Mattie felt like a galumphing elephant. But she genuinely liked Jillian, and envied her happiness and the baby that would soon arrive for her and Brody.

"Things will be fine for you, Jillian. God knows why you want him—" she grinned "—but you've got my brother now. Soon you'll be married, and he'll take good care of you and the baby." Her gaze dropped to the other woman's gently rounded abdomen, and a sigh escaped. "I envy you so. I'd like to have children. If only I could find someone to care about me the way Brody does you."

"I've loved him for so many years." Jillian's blue-green eyes always sparkled, but never more than when she mentioned her man. "I truly hope you find some-one and are as happy as I am."

"Me, too." She glanced around the room again, checking out the men. She did a double take as she saw a man who looked an awful lot like her brother crossing the room. The man was wearing Brody's frown. Behind him was none other than Dawson Pres-cott's twin. At least, she hoped it was. She couldn't be so unlucky that the two of them would show up here.

"I don't believe it," she muttered. "How could they have found me here?"

Jillian looked uneasy. "I hope you don't mind. When I went to the ladies' room—the place I spend so much time in these days," she said ruefully, "I called Brody. The corporate office is practically around the corner. I missed him and just wanted to say hello. He was in a meeting with Dawson. I told him where we were and asked him to meet us if he could.''

"Imagine that." Mattie wondered which of the gods she had offended. Why was she being punished?

"I thought they would be at the office much longer," Jillian continued. "He must have dropped everything. For me." She smiled, the expression of a woman in love. "Isn't he wonderful?"

The two men stopped at their table and looked down. Fresh from the office, they were wearing slacks and dress shirts. They stood out like Rockettes with broken legs. Worse, she was disturbed that Dawson looked as good, if not better, than he had just that morning when she'd seen him in jeans and boots. She was afraid even a burlap bag wouldn't hide his muscular frame and the masculinity that made her senses sit up and take notice.

Mattie squirmed under her brother's stare, not so much because she knew he was angry, but because Dawson was there to witness the chewing out she knew was coming. "Hi, bro," she said. "What's going on?"

"That's what I'd like to know, Matilda."

She winced, then glanced at Dawson and didn't miss the expression on his face. He was grinning. Not with his mouth, but she could see it in his eyes. On the inside, he was smiling from ear to ear. Maybe she didn't hate her name as much as the fact that when someone called her Matilda she was usually in trouble. Why, oh, why did Dawson have to be here? He already treated her as if she were twelve years old. Now he was witness to her brother treating her like a twelve-year-old delinquent.

She looked up—way up—and met Brody's gray-eyed gaze. That black hair of his and the stern look on his handsome face might intimidate some people. But not her. Caught she might be, but cornered— never.

She lifted her chin. "I'm checking out San Antonio nightlife, Brody. Your fiancée very kindly agreed to accompany me, since she knows the area."

Brody smiled at Jillian, and a person would have to be blind not to see all the love in his expression. But when he glanced her way again, Mattie squirmed. The grim look was back.

"She's pregnant, Mattie," he said. "What in the world possessed you to drag her to a place like this?"

Jillian put her hand on his arm. "She didn't drag me, Brody. She couldn't. I'm the size of a beached whale—it would take a crane to move me anywhere these days. Don't be so hard on her." Jillian linked her fingers with his. "There's nothing wrong with this place. Besides, I'm pregnant, not sick. Being here won't hurt me." She leaned forward and said, "Hi, Dawson."

He smiled. "Hi, yourself. How are you?"

"Fine, now that you guys are here. I was missing Brody a bunch."

"Can I get you ladies something to drink?" he asked.

When he met her gaze, Mattie noticed that same glint in his eyes, the one that pegged her as an amusing child. How she would love to wipe that look off his face and show him a thing or two about the woman she was.

But now wasn't the time. And since he was here, Mattie decided, he might as well make himself useful. "I'd like a glass of wine," she said.

"Sparkling water for me," Jill chimed in.

Brody glared at Mattie. "Make it two waters," he said to Dawson.

"Sweetheart," Jillian said to him, "why don't you go along with Dawson and help him carry the drinks?"

He bent over to kiss her cheek. "Whatever you say."

When the two men were gone, Mattie didn't miss the pitying look Jillian sent her way. "I'm sorry, Mattie," she said. "I wouldn't have called him if I'd known he would act that way."

"Don't worry about it. At least you're with the man you love and he makes you happy. It's just my bad luck that he acts like a mother hen." What bothered her more was Dawson's presence. He would see her big brother treating her like a kid when she was doing her best to show him she was a grown woman.

Jillian glanced over to the bar where the two men were talking while waiting for the drink order. "Your brother's intentions are good, Mattie."

"Maybe. But you know what they say about the road to hell." Dejectedly, Mattie rested her chin in her hand.

"Just you leave him to me when they come back."

Mattie watched several cowboys move around on a small dais in the corner of the room. Three picked up a couple of guitars and a fiddle, while one sat at a keyboard and another tested the microphone. Then they began to play a slow, country and western song. The words were sad, about love gone bad. Mattie had only one experience with love. Adolescent love—definitely gone bad. But she was willing to give romance

another try. How else was she going to find her soul
mate and have the family she wanted so badly?

She glanced around the room, attempting to catch
the eye of one of the unattached men present. Trying
to look available and pleasant, she plastered a smile
on her face. No one gave her a second look.

Her small window of opportunity slammed shut
when Brody and Dawson returned with the drinks. Her
brother sat next to Jillian and possessively draped his
arm across her shoulders. She snuggled into him with
a contented sigh. Dawson was forced to take the empty
chair at the table beside her, and content wasn't exactly the word Mattie would use to describe his body
language. In fact, he angled all of his very attractive
muscles as far away from her as he could get and still
remain in the same county.

But Mattie didn't miss the glances he received from
other women in the room. And the realization gave
her the strangest feeling, like the weight of a stone
sitting on her chest.

"Brody?" Jillian smiled sweetly.

"Hmm?"

"Would you dance with me?"

He gave her rounded belly a skeptical look. "Is it
all right? Not too much exertion?"

"I had more exertion last night," she said, smiling
seductively at him. He grinned—a look of supreme
male satisfaction that Mattie didn't quite understand.

"Okay, lady. Let's do it." He held out his hand,
and Jillian put her small one in his palm and let him
help her to her feet.

They walked to the dance floor without a backward
glance—as if they were the only two people in the
world. Mattie watched Brody take Jillian in his arms,

and she went willingly, resting her head against his chest. He brushed his cheek across her hair and rubbed his thumb across the back of her hand as they swayed to the music.

Mattie envied them. Would she ever have eyes for just one man and he for her? Would any man ever hold her as if she were the most precious person in his world? As if his life would be meaningless without her? She glanced around the room at all the men who kept to themselves. *Not any time soon*, she thought ruefully.

"You know Brody means well." Dawson met her gaze.

"Jillian said the same thing to me."

"She's right." He took a sip of his beer. "He cares about you."

"She said that, too. And that if she'd had brothers to watch out for her maybe she wouldn't have made mistakes in her life."

"She could be right." Dawson glanced at the couple on the dance floor.

"On the other hand, maybe those mistakes made her appreciate a good thing when she found it. How will I know unless I get a chance to live?" Mattie asked, not really expecting Dawson to answer.

"Patience, Mattie. He'll be married soon. When the baby arrives, he won't have time to keep track of you. And he'll be too tired. I understand babies have this annoying habit of eating every two or three hours, day and night."

"Annoying?" She studied him. "Don't you like kids? After the way you handled them this morning, you could have fooled me."

One corner of his mouth quirked. "Did you just pay me a compliment?"

"No way." But she couldn't help grinning back at him. "You just looked like you were having the time of your life, and the kids took to you like ducks to water. I figured you would want half a dozen."

He shook his head. "It scares the hell out of me. I'm beginning to think stability is a myth. And I wouldn't bring a baby boy into this world without a guarantee of that."

She took a sip from her glass, secretly grateful that it was water. "When my little girl comes into this world, I will welcome her with open arms. Two o'clock feedings and all."

He raised one eyebrow. "Little girl?"

"If you can have a boy, why can't I have a girl?"

He shrugged. "No reason. Especially since the way you handled those schoolkids was damn close to miraculous. I was bowled over at how you sized up each one and picked just the right horse. The whole thing went a lot more smoothly than I would have guessed. Thanks to your expertise."

"Did you just pay me a compliment?" she asked, joking because she didn't know how else to act.

"No way," he said, but the amusement in his eyes belied the words.

His praise made her glow from head to toe. Inside and out. She didn't know nice words from a man could make her feel this way. If only it had been something about how desirable she was, instead of her ability with horses. Then she would see his indifference and raise him a flirtation or two.

"What I did isn't a miracle," she said. "I've always

liked children. And I haven't made a secret of the fact that I would like to have one. Soon.''

He leveled an appraising glance around the room, then met her gaze. ''First you have to grow up, your ladyship.''

ENCHANTED MOON

As she considered her fleeting momentary glimpse he turned and flew to greet her visitor.

Victoria would change chair tonight. The room in another few hours until you were to greet all your friends.

Four

"**I** don't really look like a kid." Mattie looked at Willa and Jillian for confirmation as she pushed her salad around her plate.

It was the day after her night before. Her very unimpressive night before on the town. She was having lunch in San Antonio with her two friends after shopping for bridal dresses for Jillian's wedding. Uncle Ryan's goddaughter had accompanied them. Mattie found her easy to talk to in spite of her recently acquired doctorate in Political Science. She had free time since she wasn't due to start teaching at Texas A & M until the following semester.

After several moments, she realized no one had commented on her statement. "Do I look like a kid?" She saw the glance the two women exchanged. "Tell me the truth."

Jillian took her lemon slice from the rim of her glass and dropped it into her iced tea. "Of course you don't, Mattie."

"If I don't look too young, then I'm a two-bagger," she said.

Willa frowned. "Define 'two-bagger.'"

"I need to wear a bag over my head in public and I'm so grotesque that one isn't enough."

"Don't be ridiculous, Mattie." Jillian skewered a piece of chicken in her salad.

"Then why didn't any of the men in the bar last night approach me?" Mattie asked, looking at first one then the other of her friends.

After Dawson's remark about her growing up, she had increased her efforts to attract attention. To ditch her brother and sashay through the place by herself, she'd used the excuse of going to the ladies' room. Apparently, she'd done it once too often, because finally Brody had asked if she had a problem. Her only problem was the look of amusement she'd seen on Dawson's face. It was becoming annoyingly familiar. Somehow when he was around, she never managed to bowl him over with anything but amusement—at her expense.

There was one notable exception. He'd admired her expertise with horses. She remembered the way his compliment had made her glow. And she wanted more. She wanted him to notice her as a woman. If she could impress a sophisticated man like Dawson Prescott, surely she wouldn't have any trouble attracting the cowboy she knew would be her soul mate.

"Since I wasn't there, it's hard to know why no one approached you," Willa said. She pushed her glasses up more securely on her nose. "You're a bright, talented woman. If they were too nearsighted to notice, it's their loss."

"Thanks for trying, Willa, but I'm not buying it." Mattie leveled a look at Jillian. "You were there. If I'm not a two-bagger, maybe it was because of Brody."

The other woman shook her head. "I kept him on the dance floor and away from you as much as possible. I'm carrying around a lot of extra weight these days and still managed to dance his tootsies off until he begged for mercy. Poor guy. It was awful.''

Willa laughed. ''By the look on your face, I can tell it was a great hardship and sheer torture.''

Jillian dramatically rested the back of her hand on her forehead. ''It was just dreadful, hideous, and—'' She started laughing. ''Who am I kidding? I can't wait to be Mrs. Brody Fortune.''

Mattie sighed. ''If it wasn't because of him, then maybe it was because of Dawson. Do you think the men in the place thought we were together? A couple? And that's why no one hit on me?''

Jillian thought a minute, then shook her head. ''Not a chance. You had your arms folded over your chest. Very closed body language. And he looked like he was on high alert, guarding the world's only chocolate stash. Not to mention the fact that you hardly talked to each other, let alone exchanged longing looks. Then again, you kept dashing to the ladies' room every two minutes.'' She shook her head. ''I don't think anyone, even the relationship-challenged, would have mistaken you two for a couple.''

''Then what *is* it? What's wrong with me?'' Mattie put her fork down and crossed her arms over her chest, looking from one woman to the other.

''There's nothing wrong with you, Mattie,'' Jillian said. Then she glanced at Willa, who gave her what looked like a go-ahead nod. ''Nothing that a little makeover wouldn't cure.''

''Makeover? What do you mean?'' Mattie asked.

Willa sipped her iced tea, then said, ''She means a haircut and cosmetics lesson.''

''What good will that do?'' Mattie asked, disappointed.

"Did you ever see the movie *My Fair Lady?*" Willa asked, leaning forward.

"Yes," Mattie answered.

"Jillian and I are going to play Professor Higgins and Colonel Pickering."

"Eliza Doolittle spent a lot of time working on the way she talked," Mattie said. "If you're telling me I need to lose the accent—"

"Not on your life," Willa said. "It's adorable. A great gimmick to meet men. You just need some pizzazz. Some style to your hair and makeup to show off your assets."

"She's right, Mattie. Your features are wonderful. And women pay a lot of money to dye their hair the same color as yours. You have all the raw material to be a femme fatale. But you don't know what to do with it. Hasn't anyone ever shown you how to apply makeup?"

"My mother tried everything she could think of to clean me up. She said I would never find a husband if I didn't put on a dress once in a while." Mattie shrugged. "I was too stubborn. As much as I hate to admit it, mother may have been right."

Jillian shook her head. "I'm not sure the dress is necessary. With some sexy shaping to your hair, a little eye shadow and mascara, I don't think men will care what you're wearing. In fact, Willa and I would be wise to stand clear. In my condition it wouldn't be smart to get in the way of the male stampede."

Mattie glanced uncertainly at each of them. "I suppose it's worth a try. But I don't know where to go. What do I have to do?"

Jillian smiled and stood up, then signaled the waitress for their check. "There's a place right around the corner, just down the street from the corporate office. I found it after work one day. The hairstylist is wonderful, and they also have an esthetician.''

Mattie frowned. ''A what?''

''It's a fancy name for someone who goes to school to learn about skin care and cosmetics. Carol Donnelly is wonderful. She's going to do my makeup for the wedding. Let's drop in and see if they can squeeze you in. What do you say?''

Mattie wasn't sure whether to be excited or afraid—very afraid. But she wasn't happy with herself the way she was. If these two women whom she liked and admired thought she should change her look, then she was in. After all, what did she have to lose? If anyone laughed, she could wear a hat until her hair grew back.

Willa stood up. ''C'mon, Mattie. Aren't you finished eating yet? We have people to see, hair to cut, greasepaint to apply. And we have to do it before you chicken out.''

''Matilda Fortune, don't be a wimp. Open your eyes,'' Willa said.

''How does my hair look? Willa? Jillian? Are you afraid to tell me? Now I really do need a bag over my head. Right?''

''No guts, no glory,'' Jillian said, laughter in her voice.

Mattie opened one eye. First impression: sleek, shiny hair. Okay. She slowly opened her other eye.

''What do you think?'' the stylist asked expectantly.

Wisps of golden highlighted hair fell softly over her forehead. Layers gently framed her face and the curled-under neckline barely brushed the collar of her cotton shirt. She shook her head slightly, feeling the silky hair move. What a lovely sensation. The best part was that she *looked* pretty darn good. At least, *she* thought so. But then, she was beginning to wonder if she had any judgment.

"Well?" Jillian asked, hands on her hips. "Aren't you going to say something?"

Mattie grinned. "I guess I don't have to wear a bag over my head."

"Now there's high praise," Willa said dryly. "You look fabulous."

"I think I like it." She looked at the stylist. "But I'm sure I won't be able to make it look like this."

"You have natural wave, so all you need is a blow-dryer to give it some fullness. The cut should hold up great even if you let it air-dry straight from the shower. Just bend over, shake your head, and it will fall into place. Perfect for an outdoorsy woman like yourself."

"One down, one to go," Jillian said. "I think Carol's ready for you."

Mattie shook her head. Partly a negative response, partly because her hair felt so wonderful, loose and free. But the best part was that it did fall right back into place.

"Carol will never be ready for me," she said skeptically. She couldn't be so lucky as to have the woman turn plain-Jane Matilda Fortune into a woman that a man would look at twice.

"Wanna bet?" Jillian asked. "This time you have to keep your eyes open. She'll teach you how to do everything."

A few minutes later, Jillian and Willa waited in a nearby lounge while Mattie sat in front of a mirror surrounded by theatrical lights. Carol, a beautiful sophisticated blonde, was checking over Mattie's filled-out questionnaire. Then she pulled out creams, brushes and containers of cosmetics and went to work.

For the next hour, Mattie concentrated on everything the esthetician said. She learned about moisturizer and foundation and how to apply them for a flawless look. Learned about cosmetics and daytime versus nighttime looks.

When Carol was finished, Mattie stared at herself in the mirror. "I can't believe it's me," she said reverently. She was beginning to believe in miracles.

"You look sensational. If I do say so myself," Carol said, and stepped back.

Mattie continued to study her reflection. "If I hadn't seen it with my own eyes," she breathed, "I wouldn't have believed it possible."

Carol smiled, genuinely pleased. "Let's go show your friends."

Impulsively, Mattie jumped out of the chair and hugged the other woman. "You're a miracle worker."

The woman shook her head. "You're a beautiful woman. I just brought it out."

Mattie walked down the hall and found Jillian and Willa in the lounge, reading magazines. When she entered the room, the two women stared openmouthed and speechless for several moments. That was a miracle in itself.

Jillian blinked. "You're an absolute stunner, Mattie Fortune. I can't believe it."

"That goes double for me," Willa said. "I knew a makeover would help, but I didn't know a supermodel would be born."

"You're exaggerating," Mattie said, finding it difficult to believe, even though she so desperately wanted to.

"Only a little."

Mattie nodded. And she couldn't wait until Dawson Prescott got a look at her. She wanted to bowl him over. Only a little.

Because if she passed *his* test, she planned to go on—to find her soul mate.

Dawson had always loved spending time at the Double Crown, and today was no exception. He just wished that keeping tabs on Mattie wasn't what had brought him here. He'd used the excuse of needing to take a ride on horseback to clear his head and relax on a beautiful Saturday afternoon.

In truth, he was here to check up on Mattie, to see with his own eyes that she was okay. He'd called the previous day and been told that she was bridal shopping with Jillian and Willa. He'd congratulated himself on being off the hook for a while. How much trouble could she get into with a college professor and a pregnant bride-to-be?

But today he'd felt restless. It had been over twenty-four hours since he'd actually seen the sassy Aussie. He wished it had been that long since he'd thought about her. She had an annoying way of creeping into his mind at the weirdest times: in business meetings, in his dreams, first thing in the morning. But as he walked to the barn to find her, he reminded himself that he was just doing his duty. He would make certain that she was all right.

He needed to see that she was present and accounted for and hadn't run off with one of the cowboys. He smiled at the thought. Since Griff had left, she'd been on the prowl with little success. His grin widened as he remembered poker night. Bobby Lee and Ethan had welcomed her with less than open-armed enthusiasm. Then when she'd started winning, they couldn't get rid of her fast enough.

And at the Watering Hole, she had been as obvious as all get out, walking to the ladies' room every two minutes. He'd caught a couple of guys giving her legs the once-over. But with one look Dawson conveyed his message: Look but don't touch if you know what's good for you.

He figured he had this covert assignment wired. Griff had called to say he would be home a few days before the wedding. When he knew an exact date, he said, he would let Dawson know. But Mattie had struck out twice with men. Dawson decided the odds were in his favor that her inning would end without a score, so he had nothing to worry about on his watch. He would play the part of surrogate big brother a little while longer to the little girl from Australia.

As he drew closer to the barn, he noticed a group of cowboys standing by the corral. He wondered if there was a problem, but when laughter drifted to him, he decided not. As the bodies shifted, he noticed a woman at the center of the gathering and wondered who she was. Loose blond hair tickled her collar, but he couldn't think of any female on the ranch who wore her hair that way. His gaze lowered to her trim waist, where her shirt was tucked into worn jeans that hugged her curvy hips. Whoever she was, her figure should be registered as a lethal weapon. Then he looked lower and noticed her long, shapely legs. He'd had dreams—day and night—about those legs.

Mattie? Surrounded by men?

Increasing his pace, he arrived just in time to hear one of the cowboys say, "C'mon down to the bunkhouse later, Mattie. Ethan's plannin' to teach us a new card game.''

''I'll be there,'' she said. ''Thanks for asking.'' Her voice drifted to him. When had it turned so sweet and musical that she could play his insides like a violin?

''Hey, look who's here. How's it going, Dawson?'' Bobby Lee stuck his hand out.

Dawson took it as he glared at the four ranch hands gathered around Mattie. ''What's going on?'' he asked.

Bobby Lee frowned. ''Not much. How about you? Something wrong? You look like someone kicked your dog and stole your favorite horse, partner.''

Mattie turned to look at him. If it hadn't been for the legs that had haunted him, he probably wouldn't have recognized her. Her hair! It hung silky, sexy and loose around her face in a very flattering style. Her eyes looked bigger and grayer than he'd ever noticed before. And she was wearing lipstick! He felt like he'd been jabbed in the gut with a two-by-four, knocking the air from his lungs.

Mattie Fortune was beautiful.

When he could take his eyes off her, he got a better look at all the cowboys who were drooling over her.

''Hi, Dawson. What are you doing here?'' she asked, watching him carefully.

Pull it together, he told himself. He would give her the same story he'd used at the house when he'd arrived. ''I needed a ride to clear my head.''

''That's a wonderful idea,'' she said. ''You spend way too much time indoors playing with your numbers.''

He wanted to shoot back a clever rejoinder. But he looked at the stunning woman before him and couldn't

form a coherent thought, let alone a witty retort. And
in any case, it would be a lie. No matter how much
he might want it to be so, she wasn't a child. She was
exactly what she'd been saying she was—a full-grown
woman.

Bobby Lee shuffled his feet. "Pete, why don't you
go on into the barn and saddle up Chloe for Dawson?"

A dark-haired, blue-eyed cowboy shook his head,
then slid a glance to Mattie. "I'm on my break, boss.
Why don't you get Ricky to do it?"

"Can't." The young man looked about sixteen and
wore a hat almost as big as he was. "Sprained my
wrist. Remember?"

Bobby Lee looked around. "How about you,
Will?"

The lanky cowboy shook his head. "Chloe hates my
guts. Kept trying to nip me last time I tried to saddle
her."

"She knows you don't like her," Mattie said.

It was as if they were circling the wagons around
her. He was the guy in the black hat who planned to
carry her off. *Not in this lifetime.* Besides that, Dawson
suspected no one wanted to leave and get cut from the
herd. This assignment to watch over her had somehow
slipped from his control. That was unacceptable. Dawson knew he had to do something to get her away from
them.

When he couldn't come up with anything that didn't
make him look like a jerk, he decided to go saddle his
own horse. He would take his sweet time and hope
their breaks were over when he was through. Or that
he had a plan to put her ladyship safely under his
guard.

"Thanks all the same, fellas. But I can saddle

Chloe. Mattie likes to joke about my job. But the truth is, I've been riding for years on the Double Crown, and Chloe actually likes me.'' He gave the group of them the same look he'd used to keep the prowling cowboys at the Watering Hole away from Mattie. He prayed it would have the same result.

He moved past the group and headed to the barn. Moments later he heard footsteps behind him.

''Dawson? Wait up.''

Mattie. He breathed a sigh of relief, then turned. ''What?''

''I'm coming with you. Chloe was favoring her back leg the last time you rode her—that day we took the schoolkids riding. I checked her, but want to give it a look.''

''Okay.'' He looked over her head and didn't miss the dark looks sent his way. He wished he could tell the cowboys that when his assignment was done, they were all welcome to try their luck with Mattie—and her brother Griff. But not a day sooner.

They entered the barn, and Dawson allowed his eyes to adjust to the dimness. That only seemed to enhance his other senses. Over the scents of hay and horses, he didn't miss Mattie's fragrance. As she lifted the horse's leg for a look-see, he worked on getting his galloping pulse under control. Talk about being caught between a rock and a hard place. He was the scum of the earth for what he was thinking about her. He wanted her. But although she looked like a grown woman, she was still way too young for him—a big clue that he needed some distance. Yet he couldn't back off and let anyone else move in. Not until Griff was back.

"Would you mind if I rode with you?" Mattie asked, looking up at him.

"Not at all," he answered. His prayer was answered. He could keep her under his watchful eye without making her suspicious of his motives. "Why?"

"I can't find anything wrong with her, but I want to watch her walk."

"Okay. You can come." Odd. He was annoyed that her reason was the horse and not a desire to be with him.

But it was good news that she would be away from the lecherous cowboys and safe with him. The bad news was that she would be with him. Safe? He couldn't swear to it. Not when he had to look into her beautiful face and pretend he couldn't care less.

The best way to handle this was to make her believe he hadn't noticed the change in her. Besides, once he got used to it, surely the feelings would go away.

"Last one in the saddle is a rotten egg," he said.

"You're on."

Her sudden, sunny, stunning smile would have knocked him out of the saddle if he'd already been in one. He was brighter than the average bear, but it didn't take a mental giant to see that this was a really bad idea.

Five

"How nice that you can stay for dinner, Dawson." Aunt Lily smiled at him.

"I appreciate the invitation. Not to mention the effervescent, charming company," he answered.

Mattie realized her own feelings echoed her aunt's words, but her reasons were quite different. She and Dawson had ridden all afternoon, which normally would have put her in a wonderful mood—the riding, the fresh air, the horses. Except for the company.

Dawson Prescott unsettled her too much to produce anything even close to peace of mind. But now they were cleaned up and visiting in the great room. Her aunt sat on the sofa facing the hearth, and she and Dawson occupied chairs across from each other with a coffee table between them. A crackling blaze filled the fireplace.

Mattie felt a little crackly herself, and just a bit hot, maybe enough to spit sparks. She had spent hours with Dawson and he hadn't mentioned a single word about the difference in her appearance. Maybe he thought she looked better the other way. If he did, he was the only one, because everyone else had given her a thumbs-up on the new look. Some of the ranch hands had snapped their heads around so fast for a double take, she wondered if the local chiropractor had an epidemic of whiplash on his hands.

She grinned at the thought, but it faded fast. For some reason she didn't understand, Dawson's vote on her change carried more weight than anyone else's—probably because he'd given her such a hard time about looking like a kid. Since he was hanging around for supper, she might be able to coerce a confession from him that she looked grown-up now.

"I think Dawson has an ulterior motive for staying to dinner, Aunt Lily," Mattie said to her aunt. "Something that has nothing to do with the Fortune charm or effervescence. He told me this afternoon that his house is being redecorated, and he can't stand the chaos."

"Then by all means, you must stay," Lily said to him.

"Thank you, Lily," he said, shooting a look at Mattie that said, loudly and clearly, he wished she would mind her own business.

She just smiled smugly at him.

"You're very welcome, Dawson. In fact, if you need to move in for a while, please feel free. After all, that's why Willa is here. Thank goodness for that, or we wouldn't have the pleasure of her company. And we'd love to have the pleasure of yours." Before Mattie could speak for herself, her aunt continued, "Except tonight it's just Mattie who will have the job of entertaining you."

"What?" Mattie asked.

Her and her big mouth. She had just been having a little fun at Dawson's expense. Now he practically had an engraved invitation to move in. But she figured he wouldn't do it. After all, she was here and her presence would no doubt discourage him. Although, she had to admit, she had seen more of him in the last four days than she had since her arrival in Texas a few months before.

"Why just me?" she asked.

"We're taking Willa to that new restaurant in San Antonio and to the theater. There's a touring company in town. She's upstairs getting ready now. If it were just Ryan and me, we would cancel. But Willa—"

"Don't change your plans on my account," Dawson said. "I've heard that the show is good. Go. Have a wonderful time."

"If you're sure," she said doubtfully.

"I'd feel terrible if you canceled on my account." He leaned forward and rested his forearms on his knees.

"All right, then. And actually, I'm glad you'll be here to keep Mattie company." Lily sent him a grateful look. "I was feeling horribly guilty about leaving her alone."

There was amusement in Dawson's eyes when he looked her way, and Mattie had the urge to duck and run for cover. She knew there was a zinger in her near future.

"I'll make sure Mattie doesn't get into any trouble while you're gone," he said. "I don't mind babysitting."

Zinger, as expected. Sometimes Mattie hated when she was right. "I may be young, Dawson, but at least I wasn't raised by wolves. I'm well aware that it's not polite to talk in front of people as if they're not in the room." Mattie glanced apologetically at her aunt. "No offense, Aunt Lily. I didn't mean you."

"None taken, dear."

Dawson leaned back in his chair and rested one ankle across the opposite knee—a supremely confident pose. And very male. "Actually, I'm from the children-should-be-seen-and-not-heard school of child rearing," he shot back at her.

"You don't say," Mattie answered. *Awesome comeback, Mattie,* she said to herself. *Guess you told him, but good.* Her only excuse for dull wit was the annoying fluttering of her heart. It had started when Dawson assumed that masculine pose in the chair. It continued no matter how he moved, and wouldn't let up. Apparently she was experiencing lack of blood flow to the brain.

Dawson gave her a small—and, she thought, pitying—smile, then met her aunt's gaze again. "I'm glad to be of service in the chaperone department. Kids these days," he said shaking his head. "Can't be too careful. She might throw a wild party while the folks are gone."

Mattie considered it a moral victory that she didn't choke him. So much for making him see her as a woman. How could she get him to stop treating her like a child? What was it going to take to get his attention?

Lily laughed. "I'm sure Mattie can take care of herself. We offered to get her a ticket to the play, but she wasn't interested. But with you here, I won't feel so concerned about leaving her alone. Clint Lockhart is still on the loose after that shocking prison escape, and we can't take any chances."

"No worries, Aunt Lily. Dawson and I will take good care of the place while you're gone." She glared at him again, in case he'd missed the last one. "And no wild parties, I promise."

"Hello, everyone." Uncle Ryan walked into the great room with Willa on his left arm. He wore a charcoal-colored suit with a crisp white shirt and red tie. His goddaughter had on a black dress that seemed to hug her slender body like a second skin. "I found this sweet young thing in the hall upstairs, and she allowed me to escort her down."

"Hello, Dawson. Mattie," Willa said, blushing at Ryan's compliment.

She raised one eyebrow, and Mattie knew what she was asking. Had anyone noticed her new look? Just everyone but Dawson! she wanted to shout. Instead, she angled her head toward him and surreptitiously shook her head at her friend. Willa's mouth thinned as she frowned at him.

Mattie glanced at Dawson to see if he'd noticed, and caught him looking Willa over. Since his gaze went from her neckline to the hem of that *va-va-voom* dress, she figured he'd missed the other woman's disapproval. Her heart fell when she saw the definite gleam in his hazel eyes.

Blockhead, she thought. Apparently he was immune to the many faces of Mattie Fortune. It didn't make much difference whether it was the old outback look or the new and improved Texas temptress. He couldn't care less. The depth of her disappointment surprised her. Did she really give a darn what he thought of her?

Lily walked over to her husband and kissed his lean cheek. "You look wonderful, dear," she said.

"Not as wonderful as you, darling. You take my breath away." He took in her appearance, the red dress that showed a subtle amount of cleavage yet still managed to look sexy. "I will be the envy of every man who sees us tonight, escorting these two beautiful women."

"I envy you," Dawson said fervently.

Ryan met Mattie's gaze. "If you were going, I would need a whip and a chair to protect you from all the men, Mattie. I can't believe the difference in you."

Her cheeks grew warm. "Thank you, Uncle Ryan. You're very kind."

"No, I'm not that nice. Just honest. If I had more time, I would continue to sing your praises." He looked at his wife. "But time's a wastin'. Your carriage awaits, my lovely," he said, smiling at her.

"I'll tell you all about it, Mattie," Willa promised.

"Make yourselves at home, you two," Lily said. Ryan held out his arm, and her aunt slipped her hand into the bend of his elbow. A true gentleman, he escorted both women from the room.

Mattie sighed. Just like a fairy tale, she thought. Some day her soul mate would hold out his arm to her. He'd be a man who would notice and appreciate the trouble she went through to look nice for him. A man who didn't have his head buried in mathematical formulas and spreadsheets. A man who would be aware of the people around him and the changes they made.

When they were alone, she said to Dawson, "I'm starved. Are you ready to eat?"

"Yup. Lead the way."

She did, and found Rosita Perez in the kitchen, fussing over a salad and corn bread she'd made to go with the pot of chili bubbling on the stove.

Mattie stood behind her and sniffed. "That smells wonderful, Rosita. You must give me the recipe."

"You, niña? You can cook?" The Mexican woman smiled fondly at her, taking any real or implied sting from her words.

"Could if I had to," she said, aware that it was a

childish comeback. Dawson already thought she was just a kid; she might as well give him reason.

She broke off a corner of the bread and closed her eyes at the heavenly taste and the way it melted in her mouth. "If I live to be a hundred, I don't think I could ever learn to make anything this good."

"I was just—how do you say?—busting your chops," Rosita said, patting her arm. "You can cook. If you find a man that you care enough about to please, you would take the time." She glanced coyly at Dawson.

Mattie wouldn't hurt the woman's feelings by telling her it would be a cold day in hell before she would search for the way to Dawson's heart. In fact, she had some serious doubts about whether or not he had one. In any case, she refused to look at him. No doubt Rosita's remark had generated that infuriatingly amused expression on his face.

The housekeeper wiped her hands on her apron. "Everything is ready. I'll serve dinner for you two in the dining room now."

"Since it is just the two of us, we can eat in the kitchen. Right, Dawson?" Mattie glanced at him then.

"Fine," he said.

He stood a couple of paces behind her with his fingertips tucked into the pockets of his jeans. The long sleeves of his white shirt were rolled to just below the elbow. When her gaze lifted higher, she noticed several dark chest hairs peeking past the button closest to his neck. He looked so sexy, her heart was kicked into a trot. She wished she could get him to notice her in the same way. Just once. But she had a better chance of flapping her arms and flying to the moon.

"Kitchen it is," she said, looking down at Rosita.

"And I think you should go home to your husband. Take him some of this wonderful dinner. Although I'm sure you won his heart a long time ago, it can't hurt to remind him. You'll have him wrapped around your pinkie as quick as you can say 'chili con carne.'"

"I don't know," Rosita answered, looking doubtful.

"Mattie's right," Dawson said. "We can clean this up. Enjoy your evening with your husband."

"Sí, señor. If you're sure."

"Absolutely positive," he said. "After all, I'm a guest. Mattie's going to do all the dishes."

Mattie shook her head, disgusted at herself. She was slipping; she hadn't seen that zinger coming. But he wouldn't get away with it. "The night is young. Anything can happen," she said mysteriously.

Rosita chuckled as she hung her apron on the hook in the pantry and grabbed her sweater and purse. "Señorita Matilda, you go, girl."

"No worries," she answered, chuckling at the older woman's comment. "I'll keep him honest."

If she hadn't been looking directly at him, Mattie never would have seen the odd expression that crossed Dawson's face at her casual remark. Was he being less than honest about something? Could it be his nonchalance about her new look? Maybe he really had noticed and was pretending not to. Although, why he would do that was beyond her. But two could play that game.

They said good-night to the housekeeper and watched through the kitchen window as she got into her car. Then Mattie realized they were completely alone in the house. No horses to ride. No cowboys to talk to. No numbers to crunch. Just Dawson and her. Let him try to ignore her now.

It was pride, pure and simple. She tried not to re-member her uncle's remark about pride before a fall. Because, by gum, she would get his attention or die trying. Even the cowboys on the ranch had finally taken notice of her new haircut and makeup. They even invited her back to the poker game. That was a step in the right direction to finding her soul mate. Now if she could only figure out why it was such a badge of honor to get Dawson to recognize her as a woman.

They were in the kitchen. She could turn the heat up a degree or two. And she knew just how to go about it. She'd put on her best brown corduroy bib overalls and the cap-sleeved T-shirt that Jillian had said showed off her toned arms. Mattie decided to undo one strap. She'd seen the look in a magazine, and had the urge to see what Mr. Stuffed Shirt would do.

In Dawson's case, the term *stuffed shirt* was apt. Because his shirt was stuffed with some pretty nice muscles. When he wasn't wearing one of those ex-pensive suits, she could almost picture him herding cattle or working with the horses. The things that thought did to her heart rate could revolutionize car-diac care, she decided.

While Dawson started setting the table, Mattie ca-sually unhooked one side of her overalls and let the strap and attached metal hook hang down. Half of the bib folded over, revealing the curve of her breast en-cased in T-shirt. Before she could see his reaction, the front doorbell rang.

"I'll get it," he said.

When he came back, there was a strange, almost angry look on his face.

"Who was it?" she asked.

"Ethan."

"Really?" she said, pleased that the cowboy had come to the door. She waited for Dawson to give her the message, but he didn't say anything. "Did he have a purpose for ringing the doorbell, or was it just a case of ding-dong ditch?"

"Ding-dong what?"

"Ditch. You know. Kids do it all the time. You ring someone's doorbell, then run away."

He shook his head. "I don't think I ever played that."

She sighed. "Were you ever a child, Dawson?" She held up her hand. "Never mind. Don't answer that. You'll no doubt turn the words back on me, and I'll be sorry I asked." She realized he hadn't told her what Ethan wanted. "What did he say?"

"Who?"

She put her hands on her hips. "Ethan, of course."

"Oh." He stuck the tips of his fingers in his pockets, and took so long to answer that she wasn't sure he was going to come clean. "He said to tell you not to forget the poker game tonight."

"No worries about that," she said, pleased that the cowboy would go out of his way to remind her. "He told me earlier today that the hands usually go to town on Saturday night, but decided to have a game instead. And they thought to ask me. As if I could forget that." When Dawson mumbled something, she asked, "What did you say?"

"Just that I wish you would—" he stopped, searching for words "—put dinner on the table."

"I will when you finish setting it," she answered. "But let me give you a hand."

When she applauded, he sighed and shook his head. Then he lifted plates and bowls out of the cupboard. After setting the salad, a basket of corn bread, and the steaming pot of chili on the table, she sat down.

Dawson was about to do the same when the phone rang. "I'll get it. Stay," he commanded.

Mattie felt like the faithful family pet. *Stay?* She didn't even train horses with commands like that. Semi-annoyed—her usual mental state around Dawson—she watched him. He lifted the receiver, said hello, then asked to take a message. He hung up and joined her at the table, sitting at a right angle to her.

She spooned chili into his bowl and set it on his plate. "Who was that?" she asked.

"Bobby Lee."

He had that tone again, she noticed. The same one he'd used when Ethan had shown up at the front door: a cross between incredulity and irritation. Something told her they were about to play twenty questions again.

"What did he want?" she asked.

"You," he answered.

"I'm sitting—rather *staying* right here. I would have taken it. Why didn't you tell me?"

"Because you're eating dinner."

"Technically, not yet. But I'll ignore that. Did he say *why* he wanted me?"

Dawson had a funny, dark, almost angry look on his face. "Not really. Something about watching a video. If you want, call him back when you finish dinner."

"I'll just call him back now." She started to get up. "Did he leave the number at the bunkhouse?"

One corner of his mouth lifted as he looked far too pleased with himself. "Don't you have it?"

"No, I don't," she said, irritated. "Guess I'll just stop by and see him in case he's not going to the poker game." When he mumbled something again, she asked, "Did you just say 'over my dead body'?"

He shook his head. "I said *bread*. How do you think chili would taste over corn bread?"

"Dreadful," she answered. "And I think you ought to have your *head* examined for even thinking of it."

They started to eat, and she studied him, sliding him looks from beneath her lashes. He was scowling at the food and almost attacked it with his fork. What was wrong with him?

They hadn't taken more than a couple of bites when the doorbell rang again. This time Mattie jumped up before he could. "I'll get it."

"No, let me—" He started to rise.

"Sorry, beat you to it." She hurried through the house and opened the heavy wooden front door. The light beside it was on, illuminating the porch and the walkway beyond. But no one was there. She peered into the darkness, but couldn't see anyone.

Glancing down, Mattie saw a single red rose, and bent to pick it up. She stepped back inside and nearly bumped into Dawson.

"Who was it?" His voice was two parts annoyed, one part angry.

"No one."

"Ding-dong ditch?" he asked, half smiling.

"Not exactly. Someone left this," she answered, holding out the flower for his inspection. "I guess it must be for Willa."

He pointed to the front porch. "There's a note."

Before Mattie could make a move, he bent over to grab it up. Then he shut the door behind him and made a great show of reading the words on the paper. When he finished, all he said was "Hmm."

"Let me see." She reached for it.

He was too quick for her. "Not so fast."

She pointed an accusing finger at him. "You're lying."

"I didn't lie. You have to make a statement to do that. All I said was 'Hmm' and 'Not so fast.'" He raised one eyebrow.

"It's a lie of omission if you let me believe it's for Willa." She tried to get the note again, and he put his hand behind his back. "It's for me, isn't it."

"You're awfully nosy. Not to mention egotistical. Why would you think this is for you?"

"Because I got my hair cut and put on makeup!" She jammed her hands on her hips and glared at him. "You didn't notice?"

"Ah. Is that what's different?" he asked. "I thought there was something."

"Yes, there's something." She heard the angry pitch in her voice and couldn't seem to stop. All the patience and discipline she'd learned to use in dealing with horses went out the window when she was around this exasperating man. And no wonder. He was about as dense and observant as a mule.

He didn't say a word, just continued to stare at her with that amused expression on his face, as if he'd just become aware of the change in her.

She glared at him. "Everyone has noticed. *And* complimented me. Everyone but you. Like I said before, you need to have your eyes examined."

"Actually, if memory serves, you said I should have my head examined."

"So I did. Let me rephrase. Eyesight is the first thing to go as old age creeps up on you. You should have yours checked."

Satisfaction trickled through her at his frown. "Maybe I will," he said.

"Quit stalling, Dawson, and give me the note." She held out her hand.

"Come and get it," he said, waving it under her nose.

"*Now* who's acting like a child?" she asked.

But adrenaline and exhilaration flooded Mattie at his challenge. She felt so alive with the blood singing through her veins. Without warning, she lunged forward and tried to grab the paper, but he snatched it away. He put it behind his back again. She reached around him, got hold of his wrist and tried to pull his arm out—a failing proposition, since he was much more powerful than she.

All's fair in love and war, she thought. Fighting dirty would level the playing field. She reached out and tickled him.

He hunched forward to protect himself, allowing her to pull his arm to her chest. She held it there with one hand, while she tried to pry the paper from his grip with the other. One by one she pulled his fingers away from the note, but he was toying with her. When she just about had what she was after, he closed his hand into a fist again.

She tried to tickle him, but he grabbed her wrists and backed her up against the wall. Using the lower half of his body, he pinned her and rested both of his hands, with hers prisoner in his palms, on the wall on either side of her head. Her breathing was ragged from the exertion. So was his, she noticed. A couple of other things didn't escape her. His eyes held a dark, intense, almost hungry look as his gaze rested on her mouth. And his mouth was barely an inch from hers.

His right eyebrow lifted when he noticed that half of her overalls bib was hanging. The soft material of her T-shirt left little to the imagination, and her bosom, at least half of it, was right there. As he gazed at her, his eyes filled with a tension that she didn't understand, but something about his expression sent a thrill through her. The sensation touched her femininity.

Mattie decided every girl had to experience a first kiss. The brothers Fortune had joined ranks and kept her isolated from the opposite sex. She was five years past sweet sixteen and never been kissed. It was about damn time she knew what it felt like.

By virtue of his gender, Dawson qualified. Since there was nothing between them and never would be, if she did it all wrong, there was nothing to lose. And she would gain practice. She needed that to be able to kiss her soul mate with finesse when she found him. And Dawson was about the best-looking man she'd ever seen. So without further thinking about what she was about to do, she puckered up, leaned forward an inch and pressed her mouth to his.

His lips were soft and warm, rather pleasant, she thought. And very surprised. When he lifted his mouth from hers, a sad little sigh escaped her. He studied her for several long moments. Mattie wasn't sure what he saw in her eyes—maybe her regret that he had ended such a pleasant experience.

A moment later he mumbled, "Oh, hell."

Then he kissed her again, and there was nothing

sweet about it. He slanted his mouth across hers and took charge. Her heart hammered; blood pounded through her veins, a thunderous roar in her ears. She couldn't catch her breath and couldn't find the will to care. Never in her life had she felt anything so exciting, so hot, so wild.

He released her wrists to slide his arms behind her and pull her closer. She savored the freedom to twine her arms around his neck and lean into him. Sensations washed over her, but she didn't miss the hard ridge of his desire pressing against his jeans. A thrill went through her just before Dawson invaded her mouth with his tongue. Instantly her lower body began to throb, creating an aching need. A moan escaped her—

Dawson froze, then pulled his mouth from hers and backed away, still breathing as if he'd run a marathon. Every feminine instinct she possessed cried out in protest. What had she done wrong? He'd kissed her back. She was naive, not stupid. She knew he'd kissed her back. It was wonderful. Surely he'd felt it, too. Had she done something wrong? She couldn't imagine what, but even *she* knew a guy didn't walk away from a hot kiss like that unless there was a problem. Should she know what it was?

She gulped in air and managed to slow her breathing to something close to normal. Mattie wanted desperately to find out why he'd pulled away. But if she asked, he would know that she was a beginner. She felt too vulnerable, too raw, too exposed. The one and only time she had put her heart on the line, she'd been ridiculed.

She couldn't stand it if Dawson made fun of her. He was so convinced she was just a kid. No way would she ask him for pointers to improve her kissing

technique. But she couldn't think of anything to say
as they stood there and stared at each other, both
breathing hard. At least she had the satisfaction of
watching him struggle to draw in air, too. That was a
good thing. Right?

"So," she said, and released a long breath. "Say
something." With great effort she controlled her
voice, trying to keep it light. She thought she suc-
ceeded.

He ran a hand through his hair. "I think I'm going
to take your aunt up on her offer to stay here at the
ranch while my house is being renovated."

Six

Through a haze of out-of-control desire, Dawson studied Mattie's glazed expression, and knew the exact moment his words sank in. She blinked twice, and her gray eyes suddenly caught fire.

A pleased smile pulled at her lips, swollen from his kiss. "It was that good? You're going to hang around for more?" she asked.

He could see she was trying to act savvy and sassy, but he sensed the insecurity lurking at the edges of that grin.

More than anything he could think of at the moment, he wanted another kiss. That was exactly the reason he had to discourage her. His job was to watch over her. The cowboys on the Double Crown were showing far too much interest in her. He figured the best way to do his job was to move to the ranch.

It was his bad luck that he'd figured that out right after kissing Mattie and discovering how very much he enjoyed the experience. On a sliding scale with ten being best, Mattie Fortune was about a fifteen.

His temptation quotient had just multiplied by a hundred, and he would have to spend even more time with her fighting his baser instincts. But with Griff out of town, Brody getting ready for the wedding and Reed on his honeymoon, there was no one he could dump her on. At least, no one he could trust. The question was, just how was he going to explain his decision without A—encouraging another kiss, and B—crushing her spirit when he discouraged her from more kissing.

He took in a deep breath. "It just occurred to me that staying here while my place is being painted would be so much easier."

"Just now you were thinking all that?" she asked. "You mean while we were—you know?"

"Kissing," he answered. "Yeah. I was thinking how much I like the color of these walls. That reminded me of Lily's invitation to stay here. I think I'll take her up on it."

Mattie started pacing. "You mean to tell me you could kiss me like—" she thought for a minute "—like Burt Lancaster kissed Deborah Kerr on that beach in *From Here to Eternity,* and the whole time you were thinking about paint chips?"

"Yeah." He nodded, more determinedly than warranted. Trying to convince himself as well as her. "You could say that." *But it would be a lie.*

"So you dropped me like a hot rock because you were deciding whether or not you want Navajo white or eggshell parfait on your walls?"

"Sort of," he said. He wished Griff hadn't made him promise not to tell her what was going on. He was almost tempted to break that promise, because he hated letting her believe he was that big a jerk. Not to mention how unfair it was to her, keeping her in the dark this way.

"I guess I'll have to practice some more—work on my technique," she said.

"There's nothing wrong with the way you kiss." It had nearly caused *him* to do something they would both regret. He'd been about to carry her off to bed, and he didn't much care whose. He still wanted to, he thought, folding his arms over his chest. Then he leaned a shoulder against the front door. "It's just that this isn't the time or place. And you and I—" He shrugged, hoping she would draw the same conclusion he had: they were like oil and water.

God, this was a mess. The last thing he would ever do was use a woman and toss her aside. His father had done it to his mother, and Dawson had helped her pick up the pieces. Earlier, Mattie had asked him if he'd ever been a kid. The answer she would never hear was no. After his father left, his mom had become angry and increasingly bitter. As a boy, he'd felt more like her counselor than her son. But it had taught him to keep his own relationships superficial so that he'd never hurt anyone.

The sassy Aussie packed a powerful punch. He'd never met a woman like her, and he couldn't help being intrigued. But he would be a fool to let it go any further.

She needed a different kind of man, one who was good at relationships. He wasn't. So showing an interest, then dropping her like a hot rock, as she'd so eloquently put it, would be cavalier and cruel. He wouldn't use Mattie, knowing they couldn't have a future.

"You and me?" she asked, repeating his words. She lifted one eyebrow questioningly. "Interesting thought. Everyone needs a goal." She turned and started to walk away.

He took two steps and grabbed her arm. "And what goal would that be?" He braced himself for the answer he somehow knew he wasn't going to like.

"To make you forget about paint chips *and* your number crunching." She removed his hand from her arm.

That was two goals, but now wasn't the time to point that out. "Mattie, you need to—"

Ignoring him, she turned on her heel and headed for the kitchen.

"Wait—" Dawson started to follow, and the toe of his boot nudged something. Looking down, he saw the rose she'd dropped on the floor when she'd wrapped her arms around his neck. At least he'd made her forget to ask who'd left the rose. Unless she brought it up, he didn't plan to volunteer it was from Ethan.

Even now, the memory sent the blood rushing through his veins in a southerly direction. He was painfully hard. It had taken every ounce of his self-control not to lift her off the floor and urge her to wrap those long legs of hers around his waist—right in the foyer of her uncle's home. If that wasn't bad enough, her uncle Ryan was his friend and a man he respected more than he had his own father. And Dawson worked at the family company. How could he take advantage of the man's niece like this? Dawson figured there had to be something wrong with him to behave this way. But he couldn't seem to help himself.

More than anything, he needed to turn his back on Mattie Fortune before this crazy attraction got too hot to handle. But judging by the calls, drop-ins and secret admirers, every cowboy on the Double Crown felt the same way about Mattie that he did. And she didn't plan to do anything to discourage the attention.

That really chapped his hide.

He bent down and picked up the flower, then placed

it on the table in the foyer. He needed to stay close to her. Just until Griff got back, he amended.

He shook his head. This was nuts. His life was out of control. It had started with his promise to Griff, and had gotten worse with Mattie's new look.

Haircut plus lipstick equaled trouble.

Mattie had never been so irritated and frustrated in her whole life. It had been two weeks since she and Dawson had kissed. On the heels of that life-altering experience, he had insisted on escorting her to the poker game that same night. It had given her immense satisfaction when the ranch hands were not nearly as glad to see him as they'd been the first time. In fact, they had practically ignored him and fallen all over themselves in their attention to her.

She shook her head and angrily jammed the shovel into the muck on the stall floor. It's what she had longed for since her arrival in Texas. But the timing of all that attention was the pits. If only it had happened before she'd kissed Dawson. What the heck had she been thinking? How could she ever have believed that it would be harmless? A test? Practice?

At least Dawson hadn't laughed at her, like her one and only crush had before they'd ever gotten to the kissing stage. And Dawson hadn't taunted her with her plain-Jane nickname. He'd just been thinking about paint chips. Disgusted, she shook her head.

It had been two weeks and there hadn't been a single opportunity to follow up on her challenge to make him forget about paint.

"Perverse man," she grumbled to herself.

Every time she thought about Dawson, his arms around her, his mouth pressed to hers, she got that warm, tight feeling low in her abdomen. Then a throbbing started between her legs. She'd thought that kissing him would somehow bring her closer to her goal of finding a soul mate and creating a family. But she had discovered that kissing a man once was like trying to eat one piece of chocolate. It couldn't be done. She wanted more. What she'd gotten was a long, disappointing dry spell. And more frustration than any woman should suffer.

Not to mention questions—lots of 'em.

The most important being, would it be as much fun with another man? Oddly enough, she wasn't anxious to do the deed with anyone else. She wanted to try again with Dawson. But since she wasn't getting any younger, she had to hedge her bets. She was ready, willing and able to find a man who would assist in her research to discover if kissing just any man would be as good as it was with Dawson.

There was just one little problem. Actually, he was just under six feet tall and had some serious muscles that made him more of a *big* problem.

Dawson Prescott.

He'd moved into her brother's room at the Double Crown. Just until Griff came back, he'd said. Although there'd been some delays, he was sure the house renovations would be finished just about the same time her brother returned. On top of everything else, the man was a psychic? No one ever knew when Griff would return, let alone tried to coordinate it with redecorating.

She shoveled more stall muck into the waiting wheelbarrow. Ever since Dawson had moved to the ranch, Mattie couldn't turn around without bumping into him. He was there when she fed the horses. He dropped by during her training sessions. He turned up when she was hanging out with the other cowboys. He was always underfoot, because he was crunching his numbers right here on the ranch. He claimed to be getting more accomplished by using the phone and fax that her uncle had set up on the premises than by driving to the office in San Antonio.

There was one thing she was starting to learn about Dawson: things could always get worse. It wasn't so bad that he was sleeping in the room next to hers. But there was a bathroom in between that they shared. She could hear him taking a shower, which he seemed to take great delight in doing every night. In her own room, minding her own business, she was forced to listen to him. And listening forced her imagination into high gear. She couldn't help picturing all his manly muscles naked, wet, soapy and sleek. He was the devil in—or out of—an expensive suit.

For the rest of her life was she doomed, when she heard a shower go on, to get hot all over? Or feel the blood rush through her? Or experience a sensation at her very center that made her feel as if she would explode? Whenever a man's deep voice broke into a rendition—a very bad rendition—of Don't Fence Me In, would she want desperately to kiss him?

"Wait until I tell him he couldn't carry a tune in a duffel bag," she complained to herself.

"Who can't carry a tune?"

Dawson. Without turning around, she closed her eyes and shook her head. She wasn't in any mood to be nice to him. "For a stuffed-shirt city slicker, you sure have a knack for sneaking up on a body."

"Thank you," he said brightly. "Although you

must have been deep in thought. I made enough noise to wake the dead.''

His voice was so cheerful, she wanted to scream. She turned around, and hated the fact that her gaze automatically zeroed in on his mouth. ''That wasn't a compliment.''

''Oh. Could've fooled me.''

''Yeah, there's a lot of that going around,'' she said, thinking about his kiss. ''What are you doing here?''

He folded his arms over his chest and leaned against the metal fence. ''I was in the way up at the house.''

Here, too, she wanted to say. Her mother would've been proud of the way she held her tongue. ''What's going on up there?''

''Wedding preparations. Deliveries. Hustle. Bustle. It's starting.''

'''Bout time. The festivities are five days away. People will be arriving. Reed and Mallory are supposed to be back from their honeymoon that morning.'' She sighed and settled her chin on her gloved hand that rested on the shovel.

''That was a very thoughtful sound,'' he said. ''What brought that on?''

''I was just wondering if Griff will make it home in time for Brody and Jillian's wedding.''

''He said he would.''

That piqued her curiosity. ''When did you talk to him? Seems to me your paths wouldn't have much reason to cross.''

His fraction-of-a-second hesitation made her wonder. Then he said in a voice as smooth as a vanilla shake, ''The day he left, he stopped by the corporate offices to say goodbye to Brody. Since we were involved in a business meeting, I happened to be there.''

Mattie would swear he looked guilty, but she couldn't imagine why. Apparently her imagination only worked when it was accompanied by the sound of a running shower.

"And what did he say about coming home?" she asked.

"He said he didn't know for sure when he would be back. But he would do his best to make it home for the wedding."

She sighed again. "I hope he's all right. I worry about him with all this clandestine stuff."

"I'm sure he's fine," Dawson said. He moved away from the fence and stood in front of her. He lifted her chin with his finger and forced her to meet his gaze. "He's one of the good guys, Mattie. The good guys always win and return to hearth and home. Stiff upper lip, kiddo."

Mattie struggled with her emotional response to his touch and his words. She couldn't breathe a sigh of relief until she saw Griff again and knew for a fact he was safe and sound. With Dawson standing so close to her, her heart went into a state of serious flutter, and she could hardly breathe at all. Then his last words sank in and she realized how Dawson had just addressed her. Kiddo, indeed!

What was it going to take for him to acknowledge the fact that she was a woman?

At the rate he kept turning up, she couldn't help thinking he liked her and wanted to spend time with her. But then, he never did anything but engage in idle chitchat. Like now.

"Dawson, was there some reason you came down here?" she asked testily.

"I told you. I was in the way up at the house."

"Yeah. But this is a really big ranch. There are lots of places you could have gone to be out of the way. What are you doing right *here?*" she asked, pointing to a pile of hay and horse muck. "I might be tempted to think that you actually enjoy my company."

"What in the world would make you think that?" he answered, a half smile pulling at his attractive mouth.

"It doesn't take a doctorate to figure out that like a bad penny, you keep turning up. I can hardly turn around without bumping into you. What's that all about, if you don't want to see me?"

"There could be a couple of reasons."

"Such as?"

"I'm a masochist."

"You don't strike me as the kind of man who has a taste for suffering."

"And how *do* I strike you, exactly?"

She studied him and said seriously, "I can't shake the feeling that you've been hurt by someone."

There was a hollow, self-conscious sound to his laugh. "You know, Mattie, that horse-listening stuff only works on the horses. It's wasted on me."

"Okay." She turned away from him and jammed her shovel into the muck on the floor of the stall.

His footsteps rustled the hay behind her. "What makes you think I've been hurt?"

She shrugged as she half turned to glance at him. "A look in your eyes. The way your whole body tenses when I bring up the subject. Body language speaks louder and more eloquently, and is more revealing sometimes, than words."

"Is that so?" There was his annoying, amused look again.

How she wanted to wipe that expression off his face. She turned away. "Yes, it's so. Although," she added, unable to resist tweaking him the way he did her, "it's interesting the way you tease me about my age, call me 'kiddo,' and pretend that I'm not grown-up."

"And your point would be?"

"You're afraid to see me as a woman." She was shooting in the dark, trying to goad him.

He laughed. "Is that so? Who died and made you the resident shrink?"

"Suit yourself, Dawson. Hide from the truth. But sooner or later, you're going to have to face the fact that I am a woman. Hear me roar."

"When hell freezes over." His tone was angry. Before she could call him on it, he left her alone again.

Where was Mattie?

After dinner, Dawson had excused himself to Lily and Ryan and decided to take a look around the place. Her aunt and uncle hadn't seemed concerned about her absence. They said she frequently got caught up in work and came in late. That first night of checking up on her for Griff, they'd shared dinner because her work had kept her out.

But that was before she had blossomed into someone who looked like a supermodel-in-training, he reminded himself. Before every man on the place had noticed that she was a knockout and started beating a path to her door.

Now he had to step up his surveillance. The downside was that his excuses were getting thin. Starting with his house painting. Which had been completed a week ago. And ending with that very afternoon, when he'd claimed wedding preparations had driven him out of the big house.

He stuck his hands in his pockets and hunched his shoulders against the chilly November evening. It was a beautiful night. Stars glittered in the sky like gold dust on black velvet. He hoped Mattie wasn't enjoying it with a would-be Casanova cowboy. The thought tied him up in knots.

Because of the promise he'd made to her brother. And for no other reason.

He continued the half-mile walk to the barn, alternately hoping that's where he would find her and wondering what he would say to explain his appearance if he did.

Off the top of his head, he could think of two reasons that Griff had better get back soon. One, Dawson knew there was work piling up at the office that he couldn't handle long distance. In fact, there was a mandatory meeting with Brody the following day, and he wasn't sure how he could be in two places at once. Because no way could he leave Mattie alone.

Two, he was running out of excuses for turning up everywhere. Mattie was getting suspicious. What had she called him? Ah, yes. *A bad penny.* Good analogy, he thought. At the very least, he was a bad-penny-in-training.

For the last two weeks he'd been fighting his attraction to her. Every time he saw her, it was more difficult to keep from taking her in his arms and kissing her senseless. It would have been easier if he'd never done it. Then he would just wonder. But he *knew* the soft sweetness of her. The touch, taste and texture of her lips. Her eager, intoxicating response.

And that torturous knowledge was the main reason

for his cold showers every night. Because he knew just one small room separated him from the woman he wanted to touch and taste again. The woman who had set him on fire once, and the one he wanted to go up in flames with.

He got hard just thinking about her. Even the chill Texas night wasn't enough to cool him off.

As he got closer to the barn, he noticed the door was open and there was light coming from inside. When he went inside, the odors of hay, horses and leather assailed him. Then he heard a voice, a man's voice, followed by a female response. Definitely Mattie.

At least they're talking, he thought. But that didn't really make him feel better. A knot of anger squeezed his chest. *That means he's not kissing her.* And for good measure he called out, "Hello."

"Dawson? Is that you?" Mattie called back.

"Yeah."

He followed the voice to the far end of the building closest to the corral. Mattie stood outside Buttercup's stall. One of her legs was bent at the knee as she hooked the heel of her boot in the wooden slat of the gate. It was a blatantly feminine pose that highlighted her slender sexy thigh, and that would have made any man sit up and take notice.

Ethan was no exception. Dawson knew that as surely as he knew one plus one was two. The cowboy stood beside her, his elbow resting on the gate, his fingers a quarter of an inch from her hair, no doubt itching to touch the silky strands. The thumb of his other hand was hooked in his belt, and his fingers angled downward. All his attention was focused on the woman beside him.

If he hadn't kissed her already, Dawson thought, he was fixing to. The idea sent white-hot anger through him.

"What are you doing here so late?" he asked her.

"Ethan stopped by to help me feed the stock. We just got to talking, and time slipped away."

"I see. Hi, Ethan. How's it going?" Dawson asked, he hoped pleasantly.

"Dawson," the other man said, touching the brim of his brown felt hat. "Nice evenin', ain't it?"

"Yeah." It was a lousy evening. He could think of a hundred things he would rather be doing.

"What are you doing here?" Mattie asked him.

He was fresh out of excuses. "Looking for you."

"Really?" She sounded pleased.

He met Ethan's hostile gaze. Dawson knew the younger man was annoyed at the interruption. He looked like a stallion who was staking his claim to a mare and ready to bare his teeth and charge the competition for possession of her. Dawson recognized the expression because it matched his own feelings.

"Would you mind if I talked to Mattie alone?" he asked.

Ethan looked like he minded a lot, but said to Mattie, "That okay with you?"

She nodded. "I'll see you tomorrow."

"Count on it. 'Night," he said to her. "Dawson." His voice couldn't have been colder had it been the iceberg that took out the Titanic.

When they were alone, Mattie turned sideways and rested her elbow on the gate. "So what did you want to see me for?"

"I wondered if you'd like to go into San Antonio with me tomorrow."

"What for?"

"I have a mandatory meeting in the afternoon with your brother to go over the details of the merger between your family's business and your Uncle Ryan's. But afterward, I could take you to the Riverwalk. You haven't been there yet, have you?"

"No."

"I know a great restaurant. The food is good. So is the atmosphere. What do you say?"

"Did you just ask me for a date?" she asked, her eyes teasing, a small smile pulling at the corners of her full mouth.

"I wouldn't call it a date."

She folded her arms over her chest. "Then the answer is no."

"Excuse me?"

She frowned. "When you have your head examined, you might want to have your hearing checked at the same time."

"I heard you just fine," he said.

"So what part of 'no' didn't you understand?"

"The part where you'll go if we call it a date."

"I guess it sounds silly, but since I've been to Texas, I haven't been out on a real, honest-to-goodness date."

And even if she accompanied him tomorrow, she wouldn't be on an honest date. Because he was the slime of the earth, and he was deceiving her. But what choice did he have? He had to be at that meeting. If he left her on the ranch, there was no doubt in his mind that Ethan would move in like a buzzard on a carcass. Dawson was between a rock and a hard place. He just hoped he didn't live to regret this.

He nodded. "Okay, we can call it a date."

She grinned. "Okay, then I'll go."

Seven

"Dawson Prescott, you're the world's biggest blockhead." Jillian glared at him.

"I wasn't thinking," he sheepishly admitted.

"I just can't believe you didn't tell Mattie that Chez Vous is the fanciest restaurant in town and that she would need to wear a dress." Jillian huffed and rolled her eyes in disgust. She gently tapped his temple. "The wheel is spinning but the hamster is out to lunch."

Standing in Brody's lavish outer office at Fortune TX, Ltd., Mattie watched this exchange. Jillian was her brother's assistant as well as his fiancée, and she had decided to work until the day before her wedding, now just four days away.

Watching Jillian needle Dawson, Mattie felt both amusement and despair. She was the "she" they were discussing who didn't have a dress to wear to the fanciest restaurant in town. Dawson had driven them from the ranch in his classy BMW, and they had arrived at the office just minutes before Dawson's mandatory meeting. Jillian had demanded to see the sensational dress Mattie was going to change into for dinner at Chez Vous. Since she had made the reservation at Dawson's request, Jillian knew their destination. But Mattie hadn't brought a dress. She didn't have a dress—shabby *or* sensational.

And Jillian's tirade had begun. Mattie couldn't help feeling a little sorry for Dawson. She did think Jillian was being awfully hard on him.

"I probably should have asked him if I needed to bring anything special with me," Mattie said in his defense.

Jillian shook her head. "No way is he getting off the hook for this, Mattie. Don't you dare be nice to him or feel sorry for him. Brody will be back for the meeting, after he picks up his wedding tux. And you better watch out, Dawson. Why, he'll—"

"What?" Dawson asked, the smile on his face clear evidence that Jillian's outburst didn't bother him a bit. "Challenge me to a duel? Calculators at fifty paces?"

Jillian's glare wasn't nearly as effective when her mouth twitched, indicating she was having a hard time keeping a straight face. "This is nothing to joke about, Dawson."

"I know. And you're right about one thing. I am a blockhead." He met Mattie's gaze. "I'm really sorry. I've had a lot on my mind lately and I just wasn't thinking. It never occurred to me to mention that this place has a pretty fancy dress code."

He really did look like he felt bad for not telling her. Not that it would have mattered, Mattie thought ruefully. Her dress code was jeans. She had nothing fancy.

"No worries," she said shrugging. "We can go somewhere else." Although she couldn't help feeling a little disappointed. The idea of going to a hoity-toity restaurant with a fancy fella like Dawson just once in her life really appealed to her.

"No way are you letting Dawson off the hook," Jillian said emphatically. "The food is fabulous and it's the most expensive place in town. Besides, now Dawson owes you. He needs to pay, big time," she finished, shooting Dawson another phony glare.

"But how can I go?" Mattie asked as she surveyed her best jeans and white cotton shirt. "I don't have anything to wear."

Dawson grinned. "You're probably the only woman I know who can make that statement and be telling the truth."

"Good one, slick. Dig yourself in deeper." Jillian shook her head. "If you ever see a corporate seminar in flattery, I suggest you be first in line to sign up."

He merely grinned back at her. "I'm going to chalk this behavior up to a combination of pregnancy hormones run amok coupled with pre-wedding jitters. Because this is not the politically correct way to treat your boss."

Jillian sniffed. "Technically you're not my boss. Brody is. Although not much longer," she said, leaning back in her chair as she ruefully rubbed her rounded abdomen. "After we're married, I'm joining the ranks of the unemployed until entering the ranks of motherhood. In fact, I'm only still here to keep my sanity before the wedding."

"Yes, and you're doing a fine job of it," Dawson teased.

"I'm sorry to be so hard on you," she apologized. "I forgot that men don't realize how important just the right outfit can be to a woman."

"Yeah," Mattie said. "The right pair of jeans can make the difference between success and failure in training an impressionable young horse."

They all laughed, but inside Mattie was shaking like a bowl of semi-solidified jelly. She had no real clue about dressing properly. Overalls bad, dress good. That was about the extent of her knowledge in this situation. Her mother had tried to get her into more feminine attire. She'd threatened and bribed to no avail. Then she had settled the mother's curse on Mattie: *Put on a dress or you'll never get a husband,* her mother had said.

Mattie glanced at Dawson, so handsome in his three-piece, pin-striped navy-blue suit. Not her first or even second choice for a husband. Although he was good-looking enough to tempt a card-carrying spinster. But she and Dawson were too different. He worked in an office; she was happiest outdoors. His work clothes consisted of suits and ties. Give her a comfortable pair of jeans and scuffed, broken-in boots any day, she thought.

But right now she wasn't worried about the rest of her life. Just a simple dinner.

Mattie rested her hip on the corner of the maple reception desk where Jillian sat. Dawson stood beside her. "I agree with you that he owes me big time. And the restaurant sounds wonderful," she said. "But I still have a problem." They both looked at her. "Where am I going to get a dress on such short notice?"

"I'd offer you something from my closet," Jill said, "but I don't think we're the same size." She shot Dawson a look as she rested her hands on her rounded abdomen. "And no cracks from you about getting my clothes from Omar the tent maker."

"I wouldn't dream of it," he said angelically.

"Mattie is at least two inches taller than I am. So even my pre-pregnancy clothes wouldn't work." Jill thought for a moment, then snapped her fingers and grinned. "I know just the place. It's right around the corner. And you have to go there anyway for the last fitting on your bridesmaid's dress.''

"The bridal boutique?" Mattie said doubtfully.

The jelly that was her insides started a major bobbling. How would she know what to pick? This was Dawson Prescott—the man she was trying to convince that she was a grown-up. The embarrassment would be too awful if she chose the wrong thing. ''The bridal boutique?'' Mattie said again, her level of doubt just increased tenfold. ''It's just dinner, not the rest of my life.''

''They have lots of after-five dresses. It will be perfect,'' Jill promised. She looked at Dawson. ''And I'm sure my acting boss wouldn't mind a bit if I leave a couple of hours early and help you pick something out. Right, boss?'' She raised one eyebrow suggestively.

''My mama didn't raise a fool,'' he said. ''Anything to keep the pregnant hired help happy.'' He met Mattie's gaze. Pulling out his wallet he said, ''Take my credit card. It will make me feel better.''

''No worries,'' she said, taking it. When Jillian disappeared down the hall and into one of the offices, Mattie looked at Dawson. ''It really is all right if you want to cancel.''

He shook his head. ''This is a date. Remember?''

She certainly did. Sleep had been hard to come by the night before because she'd been so excited. She'd felt like a kid on the night before Christmas. But who knew it would be so complicated?

''We can go somewhere else,'' she said. ''What about the club we all went to that night? The Watering Hole? What I'm wearing would be fine for that.''

His eyes darkened as if he were remembering something unpleasant, then he shook his head emphatically.

"No way. I promised you fancy-schmancy, and that's what you're going to get." He raised one eyebrow, and she knew he was going to zing her. "You're not afraid of buying a dress, are you, Mattie? I promise it won't hurt a bit."

"Is that personal experience talking? Because you've worn so many?" she shot back.

Before he could retort, Jillian returned with her purse slung over her shoulder. "Dawson, you know where Brody's apartment is?" she asked.

He thought for a moment and nodded. "It's the Remington Heights building. On 3rd Avenue."

"That's the place," Jillian said. "I'm fixing dinner for him tonight. When Mattie and I are finished shopping, I'll take her with me so she can get ready. You can pick her up at seven-thirty. Sharp," she said.

He saluted. "Okay, Ma."

Mattie dutifully followed her friend to the elevator. "See you later," she called over her shoulder. She couldn't shake the feeling of being a lamb going to slaughter.

"Shut my mouth and slap me silly." Dawson stared at Mattie. "Who are you and what have you done with that sassy Australian cowgirl?"

He'd thought a haircut and lipstick were trouble. Nothing had prepared him for the one-two punch of the dress she had picked up that afternoon.

"Is it all right?" Standing in Brody's luxurious living room, she nervously glanced down, smoothing an imaginary wrinkle on the black lace covering her thigh.

He broke out in a sweat and swallowed hard.

"You'll do," he said simply, wondering if she noticed his hoarse voice.

Dawson made a circular motion with his finger, indicating she should turn. Although he had a feeling it was tantamount to shooting himself in the foot, he wanted to see her from every angle. He couldn't take his eyes off her. She'd bought a black lace sheath that hugged every one of her delicious curves, starting with just the hint of her breasts visible above the rounded neckline. The proverbial Little Black Dress.

Little was the operative word, he thought, as his gaze lowered. There wasn't enough material in the dress to cover her legs. Just past her thighs, the hem came to an abrupt halt. Not that he was complaining. But he'd thought they were a lethal weapon even encased in denim. Kissed by smoky black nylons, her gams could end the cold war. And in three-inch spike heels, they looked longer, sexier, and more shapely than even his vivid imagination could have produced.

As his gaze swept back up the fascinating length of her, he saw where some of the rest of the dress material was. Around her long, beautiful neck, she wore a choker of matching black lace. And the thought hit him: he wanted to kiss her again—starting with her full lips, lingering a while on that elegant neck, then all the way down to—

"Dawson?" Mattie cleared her throat.

"Hmm?" He shook his head to clear it of the seductive image. Had she been talking to him? "Did you say something?"

"I said I never heard that expression before. 'Shut my mouth and slap me silly.' Does it mean I look all right?" she asked. "Or will they throw me out of Chez Vous on my behind?"

"Oh, yeah," he answered.

"They'll throw me out?" She looked stricken.

He blinked. "No. I mean yes." He let out a long breath. "You look perfect. No one will throw you out of anywhere."

Although he was beginning to wish someone would throw *him* out, preferably on his head to knock some sense into him. If he could rewind the series of events that had put him here, he would have slapped himself sooner and plastered duct tape over his mouth before promising to take her somewhere that required a killer dress. A place that specialized in Texas barbecue would have been just the ticket. Where the hell was his brain? Why had it been so important to take her somewhere for which she needed to dress up like this?

But he knew the answer. He'd figured he needed something spectacular to entice her off the ranch and away from Ethan. Rumor was, she wanted a cowboy. It was Dawson's job to keep her from getting one— at least for a few more days. Therefore, he needed to lure her to his turf. The city.

But the joke was on him. Now he had to spend the evening with her looking like—oh, boy. It suddenly struck him that she'd nailed him when she'd said he was trying to keep her a kid. Somehow he'd known that if he ever acknowledged she was a full-grown woman, he would be in a lot of trouble.

Well, here he was and there she was. No way could he deny that she was all grown-up. A woman. So beautiful he ached with the need to kiss her again, feel the silk of her hair, touch all the soft curves that she'd dressed in black lace for the evening. And no way could he back out of this date. Yup, he was in a lot of trouble. Maybe he could call up reinforcements.

"Where are Brody and Jillian?" he asked. "Maybe they'd like to join us."

"They've already eaten. And she told him she was craving pistachio-nut ice cream, so he took her for some. Besides, they said something about wanting to spend some quiet time alone together because when the wedding festivities start, they won't be able to catch their breath for a while. He said to just lock the door behind us."

No help there, he thought. Taking a deep breath, he decided, damn the torpedoes and full speed ahead. The sooner the better, so he could get this over with. And to some place public enough to take the edge off the temptation she presented.

He held out his arm. "Your chariot awaits, your ladyship."

"Thank you, kind sir," she said, laughing.

The sound went straight through him, leaving a trail of fire in its path. And him in a state of readiness—and need.

Mattie heard the *crunch* of gravel beneath the tires of Dawson's BMW as he guided the luxury car to a stop near the big house on the Double Crown Ranch. He turned off the ignition. The clock on the dash said midnight, the witching hour. And a full moon bathed everything in a silver glow.

Taking a deep breath, he said, "What's the name of that perfume you're wearing? At the restaurant and all the way home I've been trying to think what it's called."

"Something Jillian loaned me. I think it's Seduction. Do you like it?" she asked. She thought she heard him groan.

"It's all right," he said.

"It's pretty pungent in a confined space on a long ride. I hope it didn't bother you."

"Nope. Not a bit," he said. But the normal teasing note was missing from his voice, leaving it curt and just this side of hoarse.

He shifted his position, as if he were uncomfortable. And she thought he groaned again. He was probably stiff after the ride back from town, she decided. Earlier that evening, she had agonized over whether or not she was doing the right thing. Using the correct fork. Presenting the proper image for such an elegant restaurant. After a glass of wine, she had relaxed enough to notice that Dawson was treating her differently. He'd never once called her kiddo, or joked about her needing a baby-sitter or being too young. Had she finally gotten his attention?

Who knew that an expensive scrap of black lace could work such a miracle?

But now she wasn't sure whether or not it was correct to thank him. He had treated her like a woman; she didn't want to make a mistake and remind him of her inexperience.

But good manners were always appropriate, her mother had often said.

"I had a wonderful time tonight, Dawson. Thank you for the date."

"You're welcome. I'm glad you enjoyed yourself. But it's getting late. Time to get you inside. I'll see you to your room." It seemed he couldn't open his door and get out fast enough.

But Mattie wasn't ready for the evening to end just yet. Tonight had been magical. And definitely a lesson in power dressing. She should have listened to her mother a long time ago. Even her inexperience with men didn't keep her from seeing that Dawson couldn't take his eyes off her. And the expression on his face took her breath away.

She couldn't remember what the best food in San Antonio tasted like. But she would never forget the look in his eyes when he first saw her dressed up. She'd wished once to see that amused look wiped off his face. And she finally had. Now she wanted to experiment to see if it might work more magic. Could she get him to kiss her again?

When Dawson opened her door, she hesitated a moment, and he held out his hand. She put hers into his palm, then swung her legs out and let him help her up. When he closed the door, she leaned against it.

"Fresh air," she said with a huge sigh. "It feels good. It's so beautiful tonight."

"Yeah. Beautiful." His voice was deep and masculine.

But what raised goose bumps on her arms was the fact that when he said that, he was looking at her. The feeling that filled her was more intoxicating than the wine she'd had with dinner. For the first time in her life, she actually *felt* beautiful. The whole evening was a fairy tale. She was like Cinderella at the ball. And Dawson her Prince Charming?

He was an awfully cute Mr. P. Charming. All evening her senses had been acute. The scent of his cologne started her insides swing-dancing. Where their bodies had brushed, or he'd touched her hand, heat had quickly followed.

And in the car on the drive back to the ranch, he'd rambled on in that deep, sexy voice of his. He'd pointed out sights of interest along the road, and she'd wondered if he was nervous. She was naive, but not dense. This was Texas, for goodness' sake. It was flat! What sights could there be? There wasn't enough variation to make it as interesting as he was trying to convince her it was. But she had responded as if he'd pointed out a new Wonder of the World. In fact, he'd had her total and complete attention, but not because of what he was saying. The seductive sound of his voice had aroused every cell and nerve in her body. She wanted him to touch her, so much so that she ached from the need.

She shivered, and her teeth chattered in the November night air before she could clamp them together.

"Are you cold?" he asked.

"A little. But I don't mind. The air feels so wonderful. I'd like to enjoy it for a few minutes." She looked at him. "But you don't have to stay." When he didn't say anything, Mattie assumed the evening was over. "Thanks again for a wonderful night, Dawson."

To her surprise, he took off his suit coat and stood in front of her. He dragged the coat around her shoulders. She breathed in the intoxicating scent of him— strong, sexy, seductive.

"Thank you," she whispered. Clearing her throat, she said, "The stars are spectacular."

He moved beside her and leaned against the car, too. Their shoulders brushed, sending sparks dancing through her.

He looked up. "It is something."

"Something? You'll turn a girl's head with that kind of sweet talk."

His deep, wonderful laugh warmed her clear through. Then she thought of something. As a girl who'd never had the opportunity to have her head turned, except for one disastrous time, Mattie wondered what Dawson had been like as a young man courting a girl.

"Dawson, will you tell me something?"

"Maybe. Depends. What do you want to know?"

"When you first started to date, what was your modus operandi?"

He looked down at her, and in the moonlight she could read the amusement on his face. She decided she liked that look and shouldn't let it bother her.

"My M.O.?" he asked. "I'm not sure I had one."

"My brothers tell me that all guys are after the same thing. They perfect the optimum line that will help them get it. What was yours?"

"I can't remember."

"Okay. You don't have to tell me."

"I would if I could." He smiled wryly. "I mean, I really can't recall dating—the early years anyway. I do remember guys who took advantage of the fact that most women want to mother a guy."

His emphasis on the word *most* convinced her that he knew at least one woman who wasn't nurturing. "Most women?" she asked.

"My mother wasn't up to the challenge. Thanks to my father."

"What happened?" she asked. It struck her that he was right about that mothering thing. She heard the pain and anger in his voice, and wanted to make it better. Isn't that what mothers were supposed to do?

"My parents divorced when I was ten," he said. "End of story."

"But—"

"You asked about my teenage technique," he interrupted her. "It wasn't very good. But none of the girls knew any better, either."

Mattie felt like one of those teenage girls. But who better to catch her up to where she should be than an experienced man? A very attractive experienced man? A very attractive, very experienced, very sexy Dawson Prescott.

"So, tell me what you can remember about your technique."

He stuck his fingertips in the pockets of his slacks and laughed as he looked up at the star-studded sky. "It wasn't very sophisticated. Pretty transparent as a matter of fact."

"Don't keep me in suspense. What was it?"

"The submarine races."

"Excuse me?"

"After I spent money on a girl—movie, dinner, that sort of thing—I would take her to what I called my 'thinking place.'"

She rolled her eyes. "Your 'thinking place'?"

"I told you it wasn't very good," he said sheepishly.

"You're right. But this is fascinating. So where was this thinking place, and what does it have to do with submarine races?"

"It was anywhere. Anywhere we could be alone to neck."

"Ah," she said. "Where do the submarine races come in?"

"There was this hill near where I lived that looked out over a valley. My buddies and I would take our dates there and park. To watch the submarine races."

"The girls must have been pretty dense to fall for that line."

"No. I usually picked the eggheads."

"Why?"

"Because they had lots of questions. Curiosity is a teenage boy's best friend."

"You are a sneaky devil."

He laughed and shook his head. "Nope. Just a guy. With my share of testosterone."

"So what happens to the testosterone when you get older?" she asked.

"Why do you ask?" he said sharply.

She shrugged. "Just curious. We've been standing out here for several minutes. Just you and me."

Mattie knew she was flirting with danger. She also knew the way a woman knows these things, that Dawson was attracted to her.

Her feelings about him were confusing, at best. If anyone had asked her a couple of days ago, she would have said she wasn't even sure she liked him. But somehow things had changed tonight. She realized that she liked him very much. She'd waited all evening to be alone with him, really alone. She'd longed for him to kiss her again. She was a grown woman who'd never known the touch of a man. Tonight, she wanted to change that.

"Yup. You and me," he said. "Can't argue with that."

"And you haven't asked me to watch the submarine races yet."

His eyes darkened, confirming her intuition about his attraction. There wasn't a hint of teasing or amusement in his gaze. The look thrilled Mattie to her core and stole the breath from her lungs.

"Do you want to go there, Mattie?"

"More than you can possibly imagine."

Eight

After spending the past few hours with the most beautiful, sexy woman he'd ever met, Dawson had little willpower left—and Mattie was testing it.

All the way back to the ranch he'd smelled her aptly named perfume, listened to the husky sound of her voice in the semidarkness, coupled with the seductive silky whisper of her nylon-clad legs brushing together each time she moved. With every breath he took and every sexy sound she made, he had reminded himself that she was too young, too vulnerable, too off-limits. But for God's sake, he was a man. He wasn't made of stone.

She had to know what she was asking. She just didn't know she was asking the wrong guy. It wasn't fair to do this to the guy who was keeping her safe from this very thing. And it was on the tip of his tongue to tell her so.

"Look, Matt, it's late. We should go in—"

In one angry movement, she pushed away from the car. "I know what you're trying to do, Dawson." She removed his jacket from around her shoulders as if it were distasteful.

"What do you mean?" he asked, trying not to notice the way she was breathing hard and what interesting things that did to the part of her breasts he could see.

"You can't pretend I'm a kid anymore."

Right on that one, he thought, opting for silence as the better part of valor.

"You just used the masculine form of my name." She handed him his jacket. "If you can't bear to touch me, just be honest."

Dawson wanted nothing more than to be honest with her. Unfortunately, it wasn't his secret to reveal. Now he had jumped from the frying pan right smack into the fire. Damn, he wished Griff would get back.

"Mattie, it's not what you think—"

"You don't have a clue what I think. But excuse me if I leave before the portion of the evening where you laugh."

She started to walk away, but he gripped her arm. "Why would you think I would do that?" he asked, angry that she had such a low opinion of him.

"I guess it's my destiny to provide amusement to men." She looked at him, and in the moonlight he saw hurt and rejection on her face. "I fell for a guy once," she said. "A major crush when I was sixteen. He worked on my family's ranch. When I managed the nerve to tell him how I felt, he laughed at me. My nickname was Plain Jane, and he didn't miss the opportunity to use it. But the worst was that he told my brothers. I'd just as soon not repeat that experience— if you don't mind."

She turned on her heel and headed for the house. He followed in her wake through the semidark interior. Lights here and there had been left on for them. It was so quiet, he figured everyone was asleep. He wanted to call out to Mattie to stop, but didn't want to wake her aunt and uncle. Finally she reached the door to her room in their isolated wing of the house. Before he could stop her, she'd stepped inside. He heard the lock *click*.

He stood there a moment, feeling like a jerk. He'd just broken every promise he'd ever made to himself. He'd hurt Mattie. Somehow he had to undo the damage he'd done. He went into the room that adjoined hers and walked through their shared bathroom. When he came out the other side, he saw Mattie still in her dress as she slipped out of her panty hose.

"We have to talk," he said.

"Good Lord!" She gasped and whirled to face him. "You've got to stop sneaking up on me."

"I didn't mean to scare you. I just couldn't end the evening like that."

"Okay. Good night. The end. The pity date is officially over." She turned away and walked over to the dresser, dropping her nylons in the top drawer.

He walked up behind her. In the mirror he saw a single tear slip down her cheek. "Mattie, there's something you need to know."

"I already know everything." She shook her head and said, "All you had to do was say so if you didn't want to kiss me."

"It's not that." He stared at the feminine curve of her neck, at the soft skin that he desperately wanted to taste.

He'd used every last ounce of willpower he possessed to hold himself in check with her outside under the stars. In fact, if he had to guess how he would reap his after-death reward, he figured his self-control tonight qualified him for sainthood. But that could change in the blink of an eye, or the meeting of mouths. If he kissed her, he knew without a doubt that all bets would be off.

He wanted her.

She made a sound that was an awful lot like a snif-fle, and he felt his insides twist. *Don't do this to me, Mattie,* he silently begged her.

"Once a plain-Jane, always—" Her voice caught.

"Mattie, that's not true. Do you really not know how beautiful you are?" He couldn't stand it that she would think that. "I wish I could have five minutes alone with the jerk who said that to you." He took her by the shoulders and turned her.

When she looked up at him with misery in her big gray eyes, he knew touching her had been the biggest mistake of his life.

And for reasons he didn't understand, he couldn't seem to care.

He cupped her face in his hands and brushed a sin-gle tear from her cheek with his thumb. Then he low-ered his mouth to hers. Her lips trembled. At the first touch of their mouths, Mattie's breathing hitched up a notch.

He lifted his head a fraction. "Don't cry, sweet-heart. Don't you see? I don't want to hurt you."

She stared at him, seeming to study the tension in his jaw, his eyes. "Then don't walk away from me," she said.

"I don't want to walk away. But there's something you need to know—"

She put her fingers over his mouth to silence him. "I already know everything I need to."

Her hands rested on his waist. She slid them up his chest and around his neck, caressing the hair at his nape. His sharp intake of breath made her smile. What-ever he'd wanted her to know was forgotten. They were in a world all their own, where everyone and everything was forgotten.

He took her face in his hands and touched his lips to hers, a brushing as gentle as the flutter of a butterfly's wings. Yet every part of her came alive at that slight contact. Rational thought washed away on a wave of desire powered by years of yearning. She didn't want to think anymore, only to feel. She found herself caught in a vortex of emotion so powerful she couldn't pull out—and didn't want to.

She felt his chest, the rapid rise and fall. His breathing was less steady than her own. Exhilaration poured through her. This is what she'd been waiting for! She wanted to touch and be touched. To give and receive. She couldn't hold back the feelings any more than she could pluck a star from the sky and cradle it in her hand.

He wrapped his arms around her and deepened the kiss. She felt his tongue trace the seam of her lips, urging them apart. When she willingly complied, he entered her mouth, and she reveled in the fact that she was taking part of his body into her own. To signal her acceptance, she touched his tongue with the tip of hers. He groaned as a shudder shook him.

Pulling back, he gulped in air, then said, "You're a witch."

"Is that good or bad?"

"Definitely good," he mumbled. "I want to make love with you," he whispered. "I want you more than I've ever wanted any woman."

"Then what's stopping you?" she asked.

He went still and met her gaze. "Are you sure? Really and truly certain? I don't want you to have any regrets."

She nodded. "I've never been more certain of anything in my life."

The corners of his mouth turned up slightly, then he kissed her and nibbled his way across her cheek to a general area just beneath her ear.

When he touched *that* spot, it was like a charge of electricity sizzled straight through her body right to her most feminine place. Liquid heat poured through her, and the result was as devastating as the mixture of water and electricity. At the same time, she felt her dress slide off her shoulders and down her body, to land in a pool around her feet.

"And you're a magician," she said, laughing nervously. "That dress came with an instruction manual."

"Where there's a will," he mumbled, tracing that spot again. "And there's definitely a will," he added, his voice husky.

In the next instant her bra loosened, and he lifted one strap from her shoulder and pulled it away. She started to lift her arms to cover her breasts.

He caught her wrists in a gentle grip. "Don't. You're beautiful inside and out."

"Okay," she said, dropping her hands. "If you say so."

"I say so because it's the honest truth."

Her eyes filled again, this time with tears of gratitude. If she'd had any doubts before, they completely disappeared with his words. She trusted Dawson. He wouldn't hurt her. She wanted him to be her first. It was absolutely and completely right.

Boldly, she unbuttoned his shirt and slipped it from his broad shoulders. Moonlight streamed through the windows of her room, and she was never more grateful for Mother Nature's light. In the silver glow, the muscles and contours of Dawson's chest took her breath away. He reached for his belt and the closure on his trousers. Mattie held her breath. She had never seen a naked man before; Dawson was her first.

When he pushed pants and briefs past his hips, his arousal sprang free. He was larger than she'd anticipated, hard and ready. Through her slight flash of fear, she registered satisfaction that he wanted her, too.

He pulled her into his arms and backed her toward the bed. He pulled down the spread and blanket, then gently lifted her. He put one knee on the mattress, then, as if she were delicate crystal, he set her in the center of the double bed. The cool sheet felt wonderful against her hot skin.

He stretched out beside her and pulled her into his arms, naked breasts against his chest. He kissed her again, and the touch of his mouth was electric. He slipped his hand down and cupped her right breast in his big palm, rubbing the pad of his thumb over her nipple. The sensation was so delicious, she held her breath to savor it. Then he shifted his body down and took her into his mouth. He suckled and laved the erect nub with his tongue until the pulse rate between her thighs seemed to vibrate to the rhythm he set.

Then he turned his attention to her other breast and took her to a higher level of wanting. She sank her fingers into his biceps and shuddered with pleasure.

Dawson slid his hand to her waist, cupping it gently before moving downward. He skimmed her abdomen, then his hand slid into the curls between her thighs. With one finger, he traced her opening. Heat radiated from her, and the throbbing at her core became more insistent. Her last conscious thought was that all her